BEST
DEBUT
SHORT
STORIES
2024

Judges

Sindya Bhanoo

Sidik Fofana

Ayşegül Savaş

CATAPULT
NEW YORK

BEST DEBUT SHORT STORIES

2024

The PEN America Dau Prize

*Edited by Kendall Storey
and Elizabeth Pankova*

BEST DEBUT SHORT STORIES 2024

Copyright © 2024 by Catapult

First Catapult edition: 2024

Please see permissions on pages 191–92 for individual credits.

ISBN: 978-1-64622-235-3

Library of Congress Control Number: 2021936334

Cover design by Nicole Caputo
Cover illustration by Sirin Thada

Catapult
New York, NY
books.catapult.co

Printed in the United States of America

10 9 8 7 6 5 4 3 2 1

CONTENTS

INTRODUCTION

A SHORT STORY IS A GLIMPSE INTO A KALEIDOSCOPE. Each one finds a way to transform the ordinary into a tightly woven miniature of human experience, where relationships, contexts, and time frames are squeezed together and configured anew, forcing out paradoxes, contradictions, and their attendant discoveries.

Before you know it, the story is over—the kaleidoscope is shaken, and a different vision emerges, composed of the same parts but entirely new in its details, characters, and conclusions. This year's anthology of PEN America Dau Prize *Best Debut Short Stories* is no exception: despite being originally published in different literary magazines and chosen without a theme in mind, the stories contained here echo and converse with one another on subjects of innocence, escape, and longing for fantasies of a future that will never come or a past that will never return.

A skilled short story writer keeps a tight grip on revelations, carefully dispensing them at moments when they've accrued the most weight. The stories in this collection often withhold information, both from their characters and from the reader, propelling us to the end and encouraging us to mind the absences as much as the words on the page. The truth lurks somewhere in the distance, appearing in overheard conversations, dreams, open windows. In Benjamin Van Voorhis's "Patience," a former military leader, now a political prisoner on a tropical island, has nothing but time to contemplate his glory and missteps, but it's a brief interaction with one of his attendants about a card game that sparks a reevaluation of his entire life.

It's fitting, then, that many of these stories explore childhood, which is lived on the threshold between ignorance and knowledge. On the one hand, children cannot fully participate in the concrete, self-aware world of adults. But it is this exact exclusion that allows them access to another world—more mystical, open, transcendent. In Josie Abugov's "Daisy the Whale," a father's failed attempt to sell an embalmed whale to a museum results in the family opening a carnival around the now-useless whale body in their backyard, complete with *Moby-Dick* readings and homemade ice cream. Through the eyes of our young narrator, we see suburban malaise and financial precarity turn into a scene reminiscent of the opening pages of *One Hundred Years of Solitude*.

Still, all children become adults, and perhaps the final death of childhood occurs when the threshold is crossed, when we know enough about the world to adopt the rigid categories and rules around which it is structured. Eventually, the narrator of "Daisy the Whale" is forced to see the magical whale for what it really is: a stinking carcass. And when it's removed from her family's yard by the state, she's left only with the image of her parents' collapsing marriage.

In Leanne Ma's "Guilty Parties," a girl and her peers at a privileged Hong Kong school are little adults from the start—concerned with fitting in, settling down, earning money. Only one of them dares to question calligraphy class and speak freely despite the consequences, and her cohort views her with pity and disdain.

Of course, most of the time, there is no clear dividing line between childhood and adulthood, between naivete and cynicism.

They often live tumultuously side by side within us, and sometimes become strange perversions of each other. Such is the case in Alex Boeden's "Alfhild," in which the titular child has a mutated irony gene, essentially turning her into a curmudgeonly old man at age five. Alfhild's father is the one with a sense of whimsy, pretending to pull treats and trinkets from her hair to her unamused response—an inversion that is irreparably destructive to their family.

In Zkara Gaillard's "A Good Word," the unknowing state of childhood is threatened by the horrors of racist violence and the cruel realities of the adult world, in which such seemingly eternal figures as parents can disappear. The mystical and ordinary blend into a terrifying vision after which the nine-year-old narrator can no longer claim full ignorance, no matter how hard her family tries to protect her.

In the bleakness of the real world, the characters of these stories search for a way out, whether material or imagined. The narrator of Winelle Felix's "Return to Sender: Big Time Tief," a young girl from Trinidad begrudgingly living in the United States with her mother staves off loneliness by shoplifting and subsequently picturing the paths her life could take given tiny changes in destiny. In Jason Baum's "Rocket," a meth addict makes a final attempt at sobriety by flying to outer space in a homemade rocket, while another addict tries to find God in the stalls of a public bathroom. Here, too, there is a childlike transformation of quotidian objects—a parachute made of old swim trunks, a space helmet constructed from a fishtank, a bag of snacks packed by Mom for the journey into another dimension.

In Annie Barnett's "What Child Is This?," weary, despairing parents to a six-year-old with a behavioral disability first content themselves with daydreams of an alternate universe where they ski and enjoy nature as a normal family. But sometimes a fantasized reality is not enough, and they find themselves escaping their son in a much more literal, potentially dangerous way.

All of the stories in this anthology contain both a portal into a beautifully rendered fictional world and a confrontation with the truth, sometimes heart wrenching and ugly, of our own.

Thank you to this year's judges, Sindya Bhanoo, Sidik Fofana, and Ayşegül Savaş, who put together a wonderful and incredibly strong anthology of debut voices. Thank you as ever to PEN America and the Robert Jensen Dau Foundation. Finally, thank you to the journals in this year's anthology, whose editors first saw the potential of these writers and brought their stories into our world: *The Cincinnati Review*, *Transition Magazine*, *The Sewanee Review*, *New England Review*, *Bellevue Literary Review*, and *Salamander*.

Kendall Storey and Elizabeth Pankova, Series Editors
Catapult

BEST
DEBUT
SHORT
STORIES
2024

Editor's Note

There is an ineffable and astonishing feeling of enchantment one experiences while reading Josie Abugov's "Daisy the Whale," a story that despite the outlandishness of its premise secured the suspension of my disbelief and earned my immense admiration from the first sentence. It begins with a madcap amateur scientist who, in 1938, is contracted by an eccentric millionaire with capturing a blue whale named Daisy and embalming it. However, the half-ton heart of this story is not the whale's but that of a family near fracture, their best-laid plans narrated by a ten-year-old daughter, who bears witness to this wondrous moment in her family's existence when it seems life might finally turn out better than any of them could have ever imagined. After Daisy is moved to the family home, her fate—as an object of study, as a cash cow, as a ticket to a higher station—becomes bound up with all their hopes, with the whole idea of possibility in America, and of the dreams, real and illusory, we are all chasing. And what is lost when they are deferred or denied.

Adam Ross, Editor
The Sewanee Review

Daisy the Whale

Josie Abugov

ONE MORNING WHEN I WAS TEN YEARS OLD, ON THE second day of summer in 1938, I looked out my window and saw a dead whale lying in our backyard. I already knew her as Daisy, and I could smell her all the way from my bedroom on the second floor. I ran down the stairs and into the yard, where Dad stood in his work clothes directing a crew of men to move Daisy into the back corner of our one-acre yard, the corner farthest from the house.

I'd visited Daisy at San Pedro before. In April, Dad's boss, Mr. Johnson, had hired some guys to go whale hunting, which wasn't considered cruel back then. They caught the biggest one they could find, and they kept all forty-five feet of her on the San Pedro Pier for a few months while they started to embalm her. This was all part of Dad's job. He was a scientist, but on the day I was born, when the nurse asked him his occupation, he said, "I am an inventor." My birth certificate, under Father Occupation, reads *inventor*.

They kept Daisy on the pier for two months. Every day, crowds would gather and take photographs and watch Dad drain Daisy of her bile and blood and other liquids, and then wince as he injected bucketfuls of embalming fluid into the crevices of her body. The whole thing smelled like eggs and chemicals. Sometime in mid-May, Dad got a call from the sheriff, who said he was going to fine

Dad and the crew because they didn't have a license to embalm a blue whale on public property.

So Dad called up Mr. Johnson, this white man he met in Arizona, the one who financed his scientific projects. For a whole lot of money from the city, Mr. Johnson had promised to fully embalm a blue whale that would stand at the entrance of the brand-new county science museum. The museum gave Mr. Johnson official supervision over the project, but Dad did all the brain work.

Mr. Johnson told Dad that getting a public license like that was one big scam and the sheriff was a real oaf, so not to worry, it would be no problem. However, Mr. Johnson couldn't relocate Daisy to his own house because it was on the top of a cliff in Malibu—even if they managed to get Daisy up there, she'd probably roll back into the ocean. But he would send over a big tow truck so Dad could pick her up and move her to our backyard in Alhambra, which was just a little town back then.

For five days, Dad anticipated the tow truck's arrival in front of our house, but he was too nervous to tell Mom: *Honey, I'm dropping off a sixty-thousand-pound whale in our backyard for who knows how long!* Can you imagine? Mom would've had a fit! When Mr. Johnson's truck finally arrived at the crack of dawn on that second day of summer, Mom was fast asleep. Dad had been pacing around the house since 4:30, full of whale-induced anxiety.

Dad woke up my half brother, Will, and took him on the drive to San Pedro that morning. Will was in high school then, but he was always skipping class to go around with friends of his in LA. Dad was trying to teach him a lesson about discipline, and I guess he thought a sunrise whale-collecting trip demonstrated the kind of grit he wanted his teenage son to have. It was still dark when they took Mr. Johnson's tow truck all the way down to the pier.

I do wonder what that drive was like, because the two of them, Dad and Will, turned out to be very mysterious men. Will had one child with a high school sweetheart, but she moved to New Mexico when the kid was a baby. Will never mentioned his son, at least not to me. He went looking for them, of course, but as far as I know he never saw them again. And Dad always said he was born in Dayton, Ohio, but at his funeral, my aunt Adele told me he grew up in Chicago. But back then, everyone lied about themselves. I shouldn't say that they lied, they just chose what they wanted to tell you and didn't include the unhappy stuff. No one ever talked to children about the racial things, and it wasn't something you would ask. That didn't mean you didn't know. Of course we knew.

In any case, Dad and Will came back with Daisy, and the other men arrived later that morning. As soon as I saw her, I dashed down the stairs. I was the youngest kid in my primary-school class and very shy back then, but I was always the happiest when it was summertime and I could be home with my family, playing in the backyard with our baby chicks and the piglets. Daisy was the cherry on top. But then I looked at Mom's face. Even as a child, I could tell she was seething. Not that she could say anything right then.

Like I said, it was a different time. Women were different. No, that's not right. They were the same, felt the same, knew the same stuff, but just couldn't say it all the time. That's not right either. Once when I was little and I couldn't fall asleep, I stepped outside, and Mom was drinking dark liquor and reading the biggest book

I'd ever seen. Whenever we'd complain about going to Mass or waiting at the salon while she got her hair pressed, she'd always say, *There's no such thing as boring things, only boring people.* She read the *California Eagle* and the *Los Angeles Times* every morning on the porch with a coffee and a cigarette. She'd left Louisiana when she was twenty with her six sisters and one brother because they couldn't get a library card down there. There were other reasons, too, but the point is, once a blue whale is already in your backyard, there's not so much you can do about it.

They put a big tent over Daisy and the men left in Mr. Johnson's truck. For a while after that, maybe a week or so, she just sat there. Dad and the crew, and sometimes Mr. Johnson, worked all day under the tent embalming her, just like they did at San Pedro, only it wasn't some kind of performance for crowds of people.

Mom stayed angry with Dad for days after Daisy arrived. When she brought him his dinner plate, she'd smack it down on the table. He liked his coffee with milk and sugar, so she'd bring it to him black. And she pretended the whale wasn't there. Back at the pier, she always seemed so curious about Daisy. She used to walk up close enough to hear the fruit flies buzzing in the folds of Daisy's belly. She'd narrow her eyes, then look up and widen them, as if she were standing in front of a great piece of art. Once, Mom took out her right hand and laid her palm on Daisy's stomach. One of the guys in the crew yelled at her to *step back, lady!* because he didn't know she was the boss's wife.

Here in the backyard, Daisy obstructed the one acre of space that Mom had. *If the whole backyard is now your office,* she said to Dad over dinner, *then maybe I'll start spending my days on the beach in Malibu or off on sailboats hunting whales.*

When Dad didn't respond to this, she added, *She's gonna kill the grass.*

But after a while, Mom's annoyance started to subside. I think she'd forgotten she actually liked having Dad around. She was used to eating breakfast with me in the morning, tending to the animals and the garden, driving into L.A. to see her sisters and the ladies she knew from Louisiana, spending a lot of time with her thoughts. I don't mean she was lonely, more that she liked to think but never grew up with the time to do it.

Dad really didn't disturb Mom's peace of mind. He was hardly some life-of-the-party guy. He knew she needed room to do her little things, so he rarely asked for favors, washed his own dishes, and left her alone when she was reading on the porch. Both of them were sort of solitary in their own way. Mom realized she didn't mind sharing her one acre of space with Dad. She started bringing trays of lemonade and cookies to the men outside. She'd stand in front of Daisy again, the way she used to at the pier. She still complained about the smell, the cocktail of formaldehyde and rotting flesh, but she liked being able to step outside and see Dad, now that he wasn't driving to and from San Pedro every day, or working all night on experiments in his makeshift office, or driving to Pasadena to study condors and airplane models.

Have I told you about Dad and his birds? Dad loved them—the larger and more predatory, the better. But he also liked carrion eaters, especially condors, the biggest vulture in North America. They flap once and suddenly they're up and away. He was convinced that the mechanics of how they fly and their proportion of wingspan to total body weight could be modeled to create a very fast and sleek airplane.

Anytime we saw a plane fly over, we'd all run outside and watch in awe. Dad would run out, too, his notebook in hand, and, after the plane disappeared from view, start writing—calculations, figures, drawings. He did the same with birds. Mr. Johnson's house sat on a hill between the mountains and the ocean, and Dad would stand by the window and gaze at the birds flying. I remember sitting on his lap in his office while he showed me bird sketches—seagulls, hawks, and buzzards—overlaid with figures and calculations I didn't understand.

This bird-plane business was the real reason Dad worked for Mr. Johnson. Mr. Johnson owned a lab in Pasadena, where he let Dad sketch his birds and airplanes, in exchange for him leading projects for Mr. Johnson. The year before, he had tested a new formula of nail polish remover that, due to a higher concentration of acetone, made doing your nails a lot more efficient. When Dad first moved to Alhambra, Mr. Johnson put him in charge of monitoring the gas tanks of five different Ford models. Back then, Dad said he felt more like a mechanic than a scientist. He liked the whale compared to some of the other assignments, at least at the beginning. Because even though Dad liked to read alone in his little office most days and spoke very little, he still got something out of everyone on the pier watching him work, then coming home to tell us kids all about the embalming process, and I think he loved imagining Daisy front and center of the new museum.

Things didn't work out like that. The museum people changed their minds and, instead of Daisy, commissioned a reconstructed dinosaur skeleton to stand at the entrance, which threw Mr. Johnson for a loop because he'd spent too much money on the whale hunting and the crew and the embalming fluid, expecting this massive return at the end.

When Dad got this news, I was eating a cookie and drinking lemonade, sitting next to him as he embalmed Daisy's thousand-pound tongue. As soon as Mr. Johnson stepped inside the tent, I could tell something was off. Dad told me to go back to the house, but I eavesdropped from right outside the flap.

Mr. Johnson promised Dad that he would find another buyer, but for now he had to pull the finances until he secured one. In the meantime, he needed Dad to keep embalming, especially if he wanted to keep working on his plane. Dad, Mr. Johnson explained, would have to fund the crew, the materials, and all the various instruments they were renting.

It's obvious now that this was the moment when things went downhill, but what you need to understand is that Mr. Johnson was truly a friend of Dad's up until that point. After Dad had left wherever he was from in the Midwest, he wound up in Arizona, where he met Will's mom on the Navajo Nation. He stayed there for years and studied chemistry, physics, and math while apprenticing for a man who ran in the same circles as Mr. Johnson, who fell in love with Dad's brain and creativity.

When Will's mom died of a beesting, Dad was too sad to stay around, but he made Mr. Johnson Will's godfather and traveled farther west to California with his toddler son. Mr. Johnson and Dad wrote letters to each other every month, and a few years later, Mr. Johnson showed up in Malibu and gave Dad a new job. Until the day my half brother died, I don't think Will ever knew his mom's name. But that's beside the point. The point is, what was

Dad supposed to say? The whale was already in our yard, and Mr. Johnson was the source of what little money we had.

At dinner that evening, things were very quiet, the kind of quiet that meant Mom and Dad were fighting. In those days, kids didn't talk about themselves all mealtime. I'd chime in if Mom or Dad said something funny or strange, but mostly, I sat and listened. Usually, mealtimes were peaceful, but that night I just eyed my rice and beans, antsy to eavesdrop on Mom and Dad after my bedtime.

I smushed my ear against the bedroom wall I shared with them. I had never heard Mom so angry, her cursing at odds with her airy voice and melodic southern drawl: *How the hell do you think we're gonna afford this? You're telling me we have to figure all this out so you can keep messing around, building a goddamn airplane?* Dad remained measured, controlled. He said, *I know, I know,* but he didn't change his mind. Eventually, Mom sighed. I heard her smoothing down the comforter on the bed. Dad asked quietly, *What are we gonna do?* Silence filled the house until Mom interrupted.

I guess we'll bring San Pedro to the yard.

Adelaide, my dad said, *what do you mean?*

We can turn the backyard into a whole carnival, charge everyone a dime to go under the tent to see the whale. She paused. *Fifteen cents for a picture. Maybe it'll even be fun.*

A few days later, a line of cars curved down our street, kids and their parents waiting to see Daisy the Whale. Dad stayed in the tent all day, still embalming Daisy with that awful-smelling fluid, but sometimes he'd look up from the task and stand for a picture with the neighbors. You should've seen just how shocked they all were that we were living in that house, way out there in the boonies, let alone that Dad was a real scientist and Mom had a college degree.

Mr. Johnson was so relieved we had sorted everything out. He looked for a buyer while we kept embalming and kept the crowds coming. He still drove to the house a few times a week. Dad always made me say hello to him, even though I thought he was very tall and scary, with his bald head and sharp eyebrows. When he came through the front door, I'd say, *Hello, Mr. Johnson*, and fidget my feet. He'd respond, *Hello, little girl*, in a big, bellowing voice.

But the carnival was wonderful. Mom, with her hair down her back, wore her poofy tea-length skirt and button-up blouse, and gave out popcorn and homemade peach ice cream to everyone waiting. As she walked down the line, five foot two and a twenty-three-inch waist and all, she told everyone about the science of embalming and all these facts about blue whales—the blue whale has the largest heart of the animal kingdom, but it beats only twice per minute. *Bump... bump*. She looked perfect, really. Every night, she took notes on Dad's notes and read marine biology textbooks that she'd checked out from the library.

The world, or at least the world from my bedroom to Daisy's tent, felt like my playground. In the mornings, before the carnival opened, Mom woke me up and we'd make ice cream and she'd ask me to quiz her on whale statistics. She was also trying to memorize *Moby-Dick*, so we'd be in the kitchen, and she would tell me, *These are times of dreamy quietude*, and what was it again, *when one would not willingly remember that this velvet paw but conceals a remorseless fang*, as we patiently spun the ice-cream maker's crank.

Dad would come into the kitchen and kiss Mom on both cheeks and then on the mouth, which I thought was so gross. And then he'd fake-scold me, with a smile on his face and his attention always a little directed at Mom. He'd put me on his shoulders, carry me outside and into the barn, and plop me down with the two piglets, where he said I belonged because I was chubby and needed a real good bath.

For the rest of his morning, before the carnival opened, Dad sat in his usual place, in the middle of the yard, and bird-watched. He'd lie on the grass and look up at the sky, his notebook and a glass of milk beside him. If a plane flew overhead, he'd stand up, as if seeing it six feet closer was going to reveal that much more of its mystery to him.

The first time I saw a group of kids from school standing in line to see Daisy, loose change and candy in their hands, shyness hit me like a bag of rocks. I ran all the way up to my bedroom. Will must have seen me, and he stopped me as I was hustling up the stairs and said that I shouldn't hole up in my room on such a sunny day. We waited by the wooden door to dodge the kids from school and then sat in the barn with the animals. He had brought some sheets of paper and colored markers, and he helped me practice drawing stick-figure portraits of our family and the animals, even though our heads were all squiggly since the ground was bumpy, packed dirt.

Will didn't leave the house that summer like he did during the school year. Sometimes his friends from the city would drive over to us and hang around Daisy. Mom and Dad went a little easier on him after they met his friends, who all seemed like good kids. Before, Mom and Dad thought Will just didn't like school and wanted to mess around, but really, I think it was hard for him to get along with the other students at the Catholic school. And I get that.

I just don't think people knew what to do with him. I mean, he was handsome and the girls loved him in a funny way. He ended up married five different times. But back then, being all mixed up like that, with a Black dad and an Indian mom who wasn't around, it confused people. And God bless him, he didn't make it any easier for them. He grew his hair down his back since it was all wavy, and whenever someone asked him why he looked the way he did and not quite like the rest of his family, he'd press them, *I don't know what you mean. No, really, what do you mean?*

But anyway, suddenly, Mom opened the barn door and there she was with all these kids from my class. I was embarrassed at first, drawing pictures on the floor with my brother and hiding from the festivities, but they looked so impressed. *You have baby chicks and a whale in your backyard?* I sort of perked up, and Mom said they could skip the line and see Daisy for free if they listened while I told them a little bit about the science of whales. She brought each of them a glass of lemonade.

Walking them around the yard and leading them under the tent, I felt like the most popular girl in primary school. You should've seen their faces—their jaws dropped like cartoon characters. Their faces crunched into grimaces at the smell—mostly chemical and artificial, but with a new hint of something else, perhaps evidence of former life. I was so accustomed to having a whale in our backyard, but then I saw Daisy through their eyes: the crisp rorqual lines along her belly, the smooth gray skin on her dorsal side, the cavernous black inside her open mouth.

When the sun set, Mom started to usher folks away. Dad had to drive to Mr. Johnson's lab in Pasadena that evening to test out some new condor theories and plane mechanics. Thinking back, and it's been almost fifty years he's been dead, I realize those were the things that gave Dad happiness—dreaming of flying and looking rather quietly at all the life happening around him.

Mr. Johnson soon disappeared. Whenever he came by the carnival, he said he was so close to getting a new buyer and joked that there's a crazy market for embalmed whale these days. But one day, Dad went to the lab after working on Daisy, and his key didn't work. He knocked and knocked. A man came out and asked what the trouble was. Dad recognized this man from inside the facility, but he forgot his name and couldn't read the tag on his lab coat. Dad explained that he worked for Mr. Johnson. *Mr. Johnson went to Hawai'i,* Dad told us the man said. *Not sure when he's coming back.* The man wouldn't allow Dad to enter the facility, not even to collect his stuff.

After that, Dad wanted nothing to do with Daisy. I thought he would've been more torn, unsure if Mr. Johnson really left for good. But Dad knew. Mom was baffled at first, then outraged. *You can't just act like you don't have kids or a job or bills to pay. We can figure something out like we did last time.* When Dad stayed silent, Mom continued. *I don't think I'm ready to close the whole thing down.*

The next day, the carnival opened as usual. Mom wore her poofy skirt and summery pink lipstick, arms wide and voice charismatic as she offered whale facts to the crowd. But Dad wasn't in the tent. He remained in his office by the barn and didn't eat dinner with us that night.

That's how it went for weeks—Mom continuing the show, Dad avoiding the maggots that began digging craters into Daisy's rotting skin. Eventually, the smell got so putrid that people stopped coming. Neighbors started talking. Mom stored the ice-cream maker in a cabinet. I'd still smush my ear up against my wall at night, but it was always quiet. Dad had begun sleeping in his office in the backyard. I no longer saw him lying on the grass in the mornings, waiting for the planes and birds to pass overhead. He didn't eat meals with us. From my window, in the evenings, I could see his makeshift desk lit by candlelight.

And then one night, I was woken by a terrific crash. I shot up from my bed in terror. I looked out my window at the commotion. In the dimness, I could see that Daisy's tent was crumpled in the back corner of the yard, and a crew of men circled the perimeter, just as they did when they'd first moved her to the back of our house. Flashlights illuminated the yard. In the middle of the grass, right where Dad watched his planes and drank his milk, Mom and Dad stood in their pajamas, buckets of embalming fluid around them. Mom was yelling at him. *Come back.* Crying. *Or just go.* Waving her arms. *Do something.*

She kicked over the buckets until the fluid puddled around her bare feet. Dad didn't move as it inched toward him. He didn't reach toward Mom. The summer breeze wrapped his T-shirt over his scrawny belly. Even in the dim moonlight, I could see he hadn't shaved in weeks.

I turned from my window and cried myself to sleep. Before I opened my eyes the next morning, I convinced myself that Dad would be working on Daisy in the backyard, and Mom and I would soon be making ice cream and trading passages from *Moby-Dick*. But when I looked through the window, I saw the Daisy-shaped impression of brown, dead grass and, where Mom and Dad had watched the destruction, a pond of embalming fluid.

Mom didn't leave her room until late that afternoon. Dad was gone—not holed up in his office, but *away* away. No one ever told me, but I knew. Will made me toast for breakfast and a peanut butter sandwich for lunch. We didn't talk much. Mom walked with pain when she cooked us dinner. For the next few days, it was so quiet you could hear every creak in the floorboards.

I don't remember if it was weeks or days after Dad left, but one morning over breakfast, Mom said she was leaving to bring him back home. She drove the beat-up car that Will took when he went to L.A. and departed before lunchtime.

Will and I waited for two days for them to return. Every hour hurt. I started to imagine Will as my new scientist-father, but then I started to cry because he didn't even like school or care about Dad's birds. I missed all the things Mom would do with me, do for me—the breakfast and the ice cream and making me feel like the most popular girl in school, even if just for a few hours. She turned our one acre of the world into a carnival. And then I started to miss the things she did that had nothing to do with me: her books I couldn't read, cigarettes I couldn't smoke, and the accent in her voice that meant she had a life before and outside of me.

I was sitting in the backyard on a hot afternoon when Mom and Dad came home. Adelaide found Dad on the San Pedro Pier, barely conscious, Will told me years later, notebooks open and the pages flapping in the summer winds. She had slapped him across the face again and again until he finally came to. When she saw he recognized her, her panic left and she was angry. Her hands stopped shaking. Her belly growled; she hadn't eaten since she'd gone looking for him. All she wanted was to rip his pages to shreds and throw them in the ocean. Instead, she stuffed them into the waist of her skirt and led Dad to Will's car. On their drive back to the house, they took turns sharing the milk she'd brought.

I was standing in the yard when Mom and Dad stumbled through the front gate. I noticed the skin on Dad's face was cracked and peeling, probably from having slept nights on the pier. I could see his bloodshot eyes. Had he spent those two days staring at the sky? Waiting for a plane to fly low enough so he didn't have to stand and squint at it? Maybe he was waiting for a condor to pick him up by his shirt and take him somewhere new. Maybe that's too hopeful.

From where I stood, I could see Mom and Dad through the kitchen window. They were holding each other and crying. If Daisy had still been there, she would have been lying right behind me. I could have turned away from the window and stared at her instead. I could have touched her belly as Mom had, counted the strange lines on her stomach, held my breath when her odor of rot threatened to sicken me. But all that remained of her was that awful patch of dead grass and, overhead, carrion birds circling.

Josie Abugov is a journalist and fiction writer. Born and raised in Los Angeles, she graduated from Harvard in 2023. She lives in New Orleans.

Editor's Note

Annie Barnett's fallible, frustrated narrator begins her day with some problems. There's an important work meeting coming up, but her good shirt is wrinkled and so is the questionnaire she has to fill out by hand. Her husband is downstairs trying to soothe their shrieking six-year-old son, her disapproving in-laws have just arrived, she's been caught in a lie, and she'll probably get a ticket for idling her car in the driveway. That's a lot for one morning, but our staff readers immediately fell in love with this story and its characters, especially the young boy, who has an acute sensory processing disorder, "a condition that the American Academy of Pediatrics and our insurance company aren't certain exists." We also loved the author's sharp, light sense of humor about everything from the new open-floor plan at the office to the chorus of angels in the school play. Every moment in this story, at once absurd and mundane, is infused with abundant humanity.

Carolyn Kuebler, Editor
New England Review

What Child Is This?

Annie Barnett

IN THE WARM AFTER-SHOWER FOG, I CONSIDER THE
questionnaire due at work today. I've had trouble with it. But because I may be hearing news about a promotion, I hung up one of
my nicer work shirts to smooth out in the humidity and spritzed
it with a fragrance that smells like the sea, and I, too, begin to
smooth out in the sea-air clouds and feel like some breakthrough
regarding the questionnaire may be coming on. Then noises begin
to carry from downstairs, where my in-laws visit with my husband
and son—distant sounds, but still they keep my nervous system at
the ready, like the low buzz of an electric dog collar, making it hard
for me to focus. My son, Aiden, is doing something my husband
and I call the Stomp. I do something odd in response. I write my
name in the fog of the bathroom mirror—*Jane*. Aiden's therapist
would call this a distraction action, or DA—acronyms abound in
child psychology. A DA is a self-preserving, often nonsensical act
intended to divert attention away from whatever is overstimulat-
ing, which for my son is everything. The Stomp, according to this
therapist, is a DA. Whatever it is, it's getting louder now. I add *was*
here next to my name in the fog.

The work questionnaire is titled "Operation 2020 Self-Inventory
and Plan of Attack." Underneath this title, there's a reminder:
Life is not a drill. After the holiday break, all managers at Motion

Innovations Inc., where I've been a mechanical engineer for ten years, will participate in Elite SEALs Management Training, led by a former Navy SEAL who now makes a living leading corporate retreats. The plan is that we are going to take the year 2020 by storm. An introduction email was sent along with the questionnaire and a video that showed the SEAL's pale, blubbery troops doing flutter kicks and running an obstacle course. We've been rolling our eyes about this retreat at work, but I've been thinking about the first question on the form for over a week: *You cannot arrive unless you know your destination. How do you see yourself in the future? Six months from now, one year, five years, ten?* The answers are to be handwritten because, according to my boss, Tad Brigador, studies show that handwriting your goals creates stronger neurological bonds, which increases the likelihood of them being achieved. The POA, as I've come to think of it, is limp with humidity now, spread out next to my husband's electric toothbrush, the blocks of white space where my answers are supposed to go empty and expectant looking.

I try to picture my future, but this is like trying to light a match that won't catch. Then an image flares—my husband and I suspended above snow-covered pines, lightly swaying in a ski lift that has unexpectedly stopped. It's a nick-of-time last run, nobody around in the late-afternoon chill, the two of us warm from skiing moguls all day, and good gear, and the promise of an après-ski drink, a seashell quiet roaring through our wool hats. Poles across our laps, we hold gloved hands, giddily nervous about the stop. We know before we feel the lift lurch back into action that we will get down safe. I have no idea where my son is in this vision—cutting pizza slices in ski school maybe, but that's ridiculous—we've tried taking him skiing the last two holiday seasons and haven't even managed to get him in his snowsuit. Aiden is simply not there. I realize that I'm not seeing the future—I am somewhere back in the past.

The image is gone. I rub the concave part of my chest—the technical term is *pectus excavatum*—a nervous habit. Sometimes I swear the hole in my chest is sinking further in. The familiar contours of the bony valley assure me it is not. I'm going to be late and begin quickly buttoning up my nice shirt, when The Stomp ends and the screaming begins. I grab my questionnaire and open the bathroom door, letting in a rush of air that causes the last of the fading sea clouds to disappear.

AFTER TOO MANY disastrous trips with Aiden, my husband, Allen, and I agreed to save ourselves the pain of traveling this year, but he hasn't entirely stuck to our plan. There's an alternate universe that Allen frequents. In it, we'd held on to my vested shares after Motion Innovations's initial public offering and are minor millionaires, like many people I came up with in the company. It's clear from the look of disbelief on his face that Allen has just returned from this land, where we live in a stone house in the old section of Cherry Creek and have a full-time nanny for our six-year-old. In our actual universe, we lacked faith in the future and sold our shares too soon, and Aiden is stmanding in the kitchen of our home in the Denver suburbs, using his heels to push the legs of his sweatpants down. Thick strands of saliva stretch unbroken across the length of his open mouth, forming a sticky web. His pants-taking-off method is terrible—erratic and wobbly. My in-laws, Dr. Thomas and Elaine Smith, see me coming down the stairs and their shoulders sag in unison, indicating that this is all my fault. It's always the mother's fault.

"Aiden," Allen says in a frustrated but resigned tone that I've come to think of as Al minor. He makes a move, stretches his arms out toward our son—a mistake. We might as well be branding him with a hot iron. We have already lost all control and will do anything to shut him up.

"Vacuum? Do you want Daddy to do vacuum with you?" Allen says. Aiden looks at us with a wild animal's wariness, chest heaving, his pants down around his ankles, yet absolutely wearing the pants in this situation. The screaming has wound down to hyperventilation, and Allen takes this opportunity to get closer to Aiden, but he can't touch him yet. Touch is one of his trigger senses. Finally, Aiden says, "Okay, Daddy," in a voice made for a juice box commercial. "Yet's go to my mat."

I notice this, but Allen thinks I'm crazy. Aiden's speech regresses after he gets his way. He has no trouble with his *L*s and *yet*. Aiden pulls up his pants and leads his father through the kitchen to the sunken living room, which is dominated by an ugly blue gymnastics mat. Our house is not a stone charmer in the old section of Cherry Creek, but it's a nice house built just like the others in our subdivision, with high ceilings, hardwood floors, and French doors leading out to a deck that gives us a view of the Rockies. The mat is a blight on an otherwise lovely living room. It was Aiden's occupational therapist's idea and is supposed to represent his safe space. Aiden has an OT to help him manage his sensory processing disorder, a condition that the American Academy of Pediatrics and our insurance company aren't certain exists. Dr. Thomas Smith, obstetrician, is not convinced either. Even I'm not totally sure SPD exists—a stance that drives my husband mad—but I don't know how else to explain what's going on with Aiden. He lies down on his back and sticks his legs up in the air. His father grabs his legs and pushes him back and forth, like a vacuum.

"Soo-ooooothing!" Aiden says, laughing. His wispy brown hair has developed static electricity from rubbing on the mat and sticks straight up. Dr. Smith shakes his head as if he's just watched a disappointing sports play. "Propweoception work feels good, Daddy." Aiden's OT taught him this. Kids with SPD have trouble when their senses are stimulated. They have trouble with all of them: taste, smell, touch, sound, sight. Even their sense of balance and their bodies' relative position in space—this is proprioception, the sixth sense. They pull at their clothes, spit out food, cover their ears when the volume of the world is not to their liking. They need to move more than other kids or stay more still. Aiden is triggered by basically everything and soothed by getting his way, or stomping, or by a push-pull or slightly pressurized feeling on his joints, which can be achieved by doing the vacuum cleaner or cocooning him in blankets—or any number of DAs. Allen's version of being cocooned in blankets is running for long distances or tending to Aiden's SPD. He is on the board of the Front Range Sensory Processing Differences Foundation and hosts a local support group.

"Is Dad pushing you too fast or too slow?" Allen asks. Aiden contemplates this. My husband hasn't even looked at me since I came downstairs.

"Faster," Aiden says. "Now slower." The doorbell rings. Aiden

startles and kicks his father hard in the arm. He scrambles back on
his mat like a crab in reverse, runs up the stairs, slams the door to
his room.

"Stan, Demitri, and Pamela know not to ring the bell," Allen
explains to his parents, annoyed. Because of our fear of an Aiden
meltdown, most of our shopping is now done online. Stan,
Demitri, and Pamela are our UPS driver, Foodie driver, and mail-
woman, respectively, but none of them has come calling. Through
the pane in our front door, I see our neighbor Lisa Simmons. The
pilled fleece scarf coiled around her neck does not hide its peri-
scopic tendencies—she cranes over my shoulder. "Good morning,
you two. You four," she says, noticing my in-laws and giving them
a little wave. "I don't want to bother you, but I noticed Jane's car
in the drive, and Teddy is on the hunt. I saw him heading west
toward Starbucks, but he might be back around."

Teddy is a local Lone Tree police officer who also happens to
live in our subdivision. He is notorious for serving his neighbors
idling tickets. My 4Runner has been idling in the driveway with
the defrost on for at least fifteen minutes—Allen turned it on for
me while I was in the shower like he always does—and there's still
a layer of ice not fully melted on the windshield. A clear snot icicle
has formed under Lisa's nose, glistening as she says, "I just thought
you'd want to know. And hey, by the way, there was a fantastic article in the *Post* last week about the environmental impact of idling.
It was pretty surprising, not to mention the data on asthma exacer-
bations. You knew my Gregory has asthma, didn't you?"

"Thanks, Lisa, much appreciated," Allen says, responding to
her question by shutting the door. In the closing wedge of natural
light, I'm alarmed to see that his under-eye area is gray and red,

traversed by blue veins under the fine skin. It looks like he has black eyes. This is the dark circle problem Allen was complaining about recently. He works from home as a lawyer and confessed to losing an entire hour of work researching the various eye creams he found in a *Men's Health* article. He deciphers complicated legal jargon but couldn't figure out which cream to buy. *Buy all of them!* I want to tell him now. We got a visit from Child Protective Services last year that we believe originated from Lisa Simmons—*child who screams and cries all the time* was the nature of the complaint, which was quickly dismissed. But the last thing we need is for Lisa to think that things have gotten physical between Allen and me. Or, God forbid, for Allen's eyes to alarm his parents. Even if they wouldn't imagine physical violence, he looks unwell. I realize I haven't even said hi to them yet.

"Elaine," I say, moving in to give my mother-in-law a peck on the cheek before she can get to me first. She wears a traffic-stopping red lipstick that stains the skin. She gets to me first. "Tom, hi, thank you guys for coming," I say, giving my father-in-law a hug. He is a trim, neat man, his body strengthened by racquetball and sensible eating. He's looked roughly the same age since I've known him, about seventy. When I met Tom, I knew that Allen would age well, and I felt confident that as long as our children did not inherit pectus excavatum, our gene pools would mix nicely. "How was the trip in?"

"Cold," Tom says. "It was five degrees in Eden Prairie yesterday morning. It's practically balmy here."

"It's seventy-eight and sunny in Palm Beach today," Elaine says. The Smiths spend every Christmas holiday at their place in Palm Beach, but now they grudgingly come to Denver for a few days first to see their only grandson, who is non-transportable. For the last three years, since Aiden started pre-K at Denver Day School, it's become a Smith family tradition to visit the campus for the holiday play so that Dr. and Mrs. Smith can have a good look at their investment. This is followed by dinner at Morton's, during which Dr. Smith asks how much the check for second semester tuition should be written out for. Mrs. Smith will usually pull the checkbook from her purse after appetizers, the longest the dinners have ever lasted because of our son. Dr. Smith writes the tuition check out at the table. Allen and I do fine, but we can't afford all of Aiden's specialists *and* college tuition for a first grader, which is what the price of Denver Day basically works out to. It's Allen who thinks that the school's specialized attention is giving Aiden his only chance at life, but I'm the one who started it, convinced as much by several of my colleagues. It hasn't seemed to help, I point out all the time, but we're terrified of making a change, of God forbid, his behavior getting worse. Now I'm just afraid that soon we won't have a choice—we've been called in for several one-on-ones with the principal this year. Even Denver Day's pricey patience is wearing thin.

"I hate responding to anything Lisa Simmons says, but I better deal with my car," I say, desperate to get some air. I head for the fruit basket, where I keep my keys, and see why my husband has not really looked at me since I came downstairs. Smoothed out and held down on one corner by a VAIL LIKE NO PLACE ON EARTH mug from a failed ski trip with Aiden last year is a receipt from The Rooster—my safe place, my blue mat. It must have fallen from my pocket. The Rooster is a bar that I pass on my way home from work. Converted from an old Pizza Hut located on an access road that was cut off from meaningful traffic when the southbound I-25 was rerouted, it's a squat brown building with the red-shingled roof shaped like an oven hood still in place, the faded outline of the words PIZZA HUT still visible from where the name was removed from the peak, and an ample parking lot, usually near empty. The owner went to Cabo San Lucas, and his sister has been covering for him. There were three of us in the place the other night, and she kept forgetting our drinks. That she remembered to give me a receipt—I've never once gotten a receipt from The Rooster—is shocking.

"We were just getting going, too." The Smiths insist on staying down the road at the DoubleTree, despite our spare bedroom. "We're going to get some breakfast before it closes," Dr. Smith says.

"It's included in our room," Mrs. Smith says, rummaging in her Chanel bag for the rental keys. I've noticed that they have a bandwidth of about twenty Aiden minutes before they need a break.

As Allen walks his parents to the door, I head for my briefcase, thinking for a second that I'll grab that receipt, hoping my husband hasn't taken a good look at it. He's a lawyer—of course he has. Allen has come back inside and notices me eyeing it. He slips the evidence from beneath the mug and waves it in my face.

"Three Sunning Dog Ales and two Moscow mules? This is from Tuesday at 9:07." I told him I was working late that night on the project that will hopefully earn me a promotion. "What the fuck, Jane? Who were you with?"

"Myself, I swear!" I am having an affair, but I'm also telling the truth. I always go to The Rooster alone, usually right after work for a drink before I go home, but Tuesday I—well, I just didn't want to go home. Couldn't make myself do it.

"You didn't drink five drinks by yourself." He's right. I drank four. The fifth I bought for an old-timer who always roosts next to me at the bar. He turned me on to the Moscow mule. I think of my accidental date's peanut-dusted whiskers dipping into his copper mug.

"I'm sorry, Al," I say. "You're right, there was a nice old guy who looked down on his luck sitting next to me, and I bought him a few drinks. It's the holidays. I did work late, but I was just so stressed about my train door project. I only stopped for a little bit. I didn't want to bring all that nervous energy home." We are very sensitive about doing anything that could possibly disturb Aiden's energy, and I'm hoping this tactic will work because I'm lying now. I left my office at 4:55 and drank one drink an hour for the next four hours.

The mere notion of disturbing Aiden's energy has disarmed my husband. His voice is less angry, more tired, when he says, "You left me alone all night with . . ." He doesn't even say his name, just motions helplessly upstairs. He's not as worried about me going out drinking with other men as he is about being left to fend for himself all night with Aiden.

"I'm sorry," I say, not lying.

"Okay, then, believe me we are going to talk about this later, but I have to get him to school. We have the thing tonight," he says in a way that sounds like he will go on repeating a never-ending list. *We have the thing tonight, and then, and then, and then* . . . He has gotten overheated and removes his fleece, ties it around his waist. His arm is bright red where Aiden kicked him. I decide my husband has taken enough abuse for the day. "I'll go get him ready for school," I say.

One thing I don't understand is how, if my son is so sensitive to sounds and lights, he can stand video games. But there he is, frog-legged on his beanbag, playing Wii. We have no restrictions on the Wii—he's allowed to play it whenever the hell he wants. He refuses a human babysitter, so we have hired Wii.

"Come on, sweetheart, it's time for school." He doesn't look up from the screen. "Aiden, please. This is not a request. Tonight is your big night, and you can't be late for school. You have rehearsals today." Aiden is surprisingly merciful. He agrees to wear his nice sweatpants—they're khaki with faux pleats, belt loops, and a zipper airbrushed onto them. He can't stand the feel of most clothing, so is almost always in sweatpants. He checks his T-shirt to make sure he doesn't feel any remnants of the tag we cut out and makes me do the same. We do the same thing with his tiny fleece. He puts on his Uggs, which thank God he loves, because most of the time he refuses to wear socks. He lets me calm his static with a wet comb and even lets me carry him down the stairs—and along the way, he nestles his head against mine and says, "I love you, Mommy." Every muscle in my body softens. He lets me kiss his cheek.

"I love you too, Aiden."

Allen is waiting for us in the kitchen with Aiden's lunch bag and a white angel costume on a hanger. He sewed it himself with a type of cotton fabric that Aiden likes, and the thought of seeing him hunched over the sewing machine, following the angel costume pattern, makes me rub the center of my chest.

"Oh, you look so handsome, Aiden," Allen says. We share a brief smile. We can't help ourselves. When any little thing goes well with him, even something as small as getting dressed for school, we indulge.

"I want to check it for tags, Dad," he says.

"Daddy made it himself. It doesn't have any tags," I explain. He squirms in my arms. He's small for his age but hard to carry. When I let him down, he runs over to the costume and reaches up. Allen carefully takes it off the hanger and shows him—look, no tags.

"Do you like it?" Allen asks.

Aiden buries his head in his father's leg, but we can see he's smiling. "Yes, I yike it."

"Do you remember your line?" I ask.

"Don't be afraid," he says.

This makes Allen so happy, he almost gives Aiden a hug without asking for permission first. He looks at me as he embraces our son, and I plead for forgiveness with my eyes before I slip out the door.

I'd forgotten about my car. The ice is fully melted, and there's a soggy ticket tucked under the wiper blade—an idling citation, courtesy of Officer Teddy. We have plenty of room in our garage, but Aiden hates the sound of the garage door opening, so I just leave my car outside. It's been on for an hour in the driveway this morning, sending up clouds of exhaust.

THE WINDSOR ESTATES Apartments are located on a wide stretch of flatland across from greater Denver's southernmost light rail station, the Lone Tree stop. It's Chain-Store City—down the road, a flagship Home Depot reliably slows traffic. Lone Tree was incorporated in 1995, and for the most part, the architecture embraces the city's newness. There is no shortage of clean lines— there's a nationwide obsession with clean lines—but there are a few apartment buildings across from the light rail station that have attempted to infuse an established feel to their buildings, their facades done up with flourishes of Victorian or English manor. At the entrance to Windsor Estates, there's a wrought-iron gate that remains open at all times. The entryway leads to a welcoming clubhouse that looks like it could be blown down in a strong wind; it sports large, arched windows through which I see a young couple sitting in high-backed chairs covered in a fabric that features hunting scenes, leaning close together to review a stack of papers. Old-fashioned streetlights parade past the manufactured-stone and clapboard buildings, distinguishable only by their assigned letter. Bill lives in building M.

I've worked with Bill since I started at Motion Innovations Inc. Motion Innovations makes motors and motion detector devices used in everything from military fighter jets to elevators. Bill is in charge of the ATV and motorized scooter department, while I am in charge of dialysis machines and IV pumps, although I hope to soon add train door motors to my roster. I've been sleeping with Bill for a little over a year, but I'm here today to end it. Bill started his annual holiday staycation earlier this week, and I know that he will be home, listening to records and getting stoned. The corporate SEALs form, crinkled with a brittle texture from being exposed to the humidity in the bathroom, is on the seat next to me, asking me about my future. The SEAL's intro email encouraged honest answers, but sitting in Bill's parking lot, I suddenly have a dream for my future too precious to share. I see Allen, Aiden, and me sometime in the distance, tired and happy after a long day on the slopes, still in our ski pants. Aiden has grown taller than his father, and although I can't clearly picture his young-man's face, I know he is smiling as he leads us through a busy crowd with ease, to our seats by the fireplace. We clink our steaming mugs of hot chocolate, toasting to something—the future, maybe. I imagine this the way you make a wish before you blow out your birthday candles, but I need to seal it with something. And just like blowing out candles is a symbolic act, something you do after the really important part, I seal my vision by turning my briefcase on its side to use as a table so that I can write: *In the next six months, I see myself as the conductor of the train door department.* It looks so pathetic, sloppily written on the ruined form, but it's a worthy goal, even if not my most fervent. I've worked hard to develop a new train door motor for Baybridge Industries, the nation's largest manufacturer of light rail train cars, and I need a win at work. I also need to start the new year with this affair behind me.

When Bill answers the door, "Can't You Hear Me Knocking" is playing—he has *Sticky Fingers* on vinyl.

"It's my lucky day," he says. "What's that on your cheek?" I swipe at my cheek, unsure. "It's red," he says. My mother-in-law's lipstick.

Bill has really great blue eyes with huge dark brows but almost no hair on his head, and something we in the field affectionately call the engineer sneer, a permanent grimace caused by neck pain. And he's fucking funny. And he is wearing an old flannel shirt that smells like aftershave and doesn't quite hide his gut, his jeans so worn I can see the outline where his wallet sits in his pocket. I can see right through his living room to the bedroom, where the swirl of the tapestry hanging above his bed—it's a nice one, a grown-up version, handmade from a weaver in Oregon—hypnotizes me. It's like an adult dorm room, and suddenly I want to go back to school, where I have not a care in the fucking world.

Then I'm in his bed, and Bill is doing a signature sex move he invented for me, inspired by my work in the IV department, called the Peristaltic Pump, followed by something new, for good luck, called the Choo Choo Train, and we are laughing. I notice the blue-green veins that erupted all over my legs when I was pregnant with Aiden, there for life it seems. And then, because Bill also sold out too early, we stare at the ceiling, bitching about the shares. Most of our relationship is built on bitching about the shares, although I don't know what Bill would have done with a windfall. As far as I can tell, he buys only pot and records. He is single and has always lived in a modest apartment, never wanted the responsibility of a house. Bill gets out of bed naked and moves the needle back on the record player. We smoke weed, a little roach he has left on his bedside table. He gets up again, naked still, to get some more. It's the legal stuff from Maggie's Farmhouse, and it's wrapped in plastic packaging that we can't get open, making me miss the good old days. Bill can't find scissors but keeps looking anyway, so I get up, naked, to get a knife, and I cut myself—not on the knife, but on the edge of the plastic that I've sawed apart.

"Shit!" Bill grabs a paper towel, and I wrap my finger in it. We free the weed and blow smoke at the ceiling. I understand the plastic wrapping now—this stuff is strong.

"I have to stay a little bit longer. I can't go in like this," I say.

"Stay a little bit longer."

"That's what I said. Shit, I'm still bleeding," I say, peeking under the stained paper towel.

"Let me see that," Bill says. "It's a scratch. Gimme." He takes my finger and sticks it in his mouth, sucks my blood. I let him. A hot-cold feeling runs through all the nerves in my body, a wave of soberness. This is bad. This seems worse than all the other things I've done. I sit on the edge of the bed and steady myself for a moment.

"Everything okay?" he asks. His hand is on my back; mine is nestled in the hole in my chest, where I keep it until the bleeding stops.

"I have to get to work." I get dressed and button up my nice shirt for the second time today. It is all wrinkled.

THIS IS THE last day of work before our office closes for the holiday season, a schedule that's coordinated with the Denver Day School, since many employees at Motion Innovations Inc. have kids who go there. It's a funny schedule this year—off for a weekend, then back for one day before the break begins—and the result is an unusual amount of restless energy that flows undammed through our open-concept office space. One of our founding partners—my boss, Tad—decided to tear down the walls after we went public, and now, where there once was a regular office space with doors and cubicles, there is a sea of people sitting elbow-to-elbow at long tables grouped together in what we call pods. Tad was wrong to tear down the walls. If Aiden hadn't been conceived before the redesign, I might suspect that the environment had affected the fetus, the sensory overload seeping into Aiden's DNA. Tad hates it, too, I can tell. He is constantly smiling and looks about ten years older than he did when there were walls. Actually, Tad has walls, but you can see right through them. He sits in what is essentially a glass box in the middle of the action.

I knock on the glass. Tad looks startled. I understand that he really did not see me. He has become desensitized. Already the collaborative workspace is a cacophony, made worse because Andre in motorboats is working with his team by tossing a mini beach ball back and forth as they say their ideas out loud. Andre is one of those who held on to his vested shares long enough to make serious money. We were warned in an HR meeting never to discuss our personal finances related to the IPO, but there's no need to discuss it—those who did well have grown their hair long, moved to the old section of Cherry Creek, and started new pet projects. Andre started the motorboat department since he now has five of them and is obsessed.

The sobering rush of regret has worn off, and I'm somewhat high again. I've floated through this whole scene and have arrived at the glass box as if delivered by one of those moving sidewalks at the airport. Tad waves me in and pushes a stack of Malcolm Gladwell books a couple of inches over, inviting me to sit down. "Jane, it's good to see you."

I blink. My reaction time is a bit slowed. "Tad, you literally see me all day long." Not too stoned to take a dig at the open-concept office space.

"How are you?" His hand gravitates toward the cover of *The Tipping Point*, which he's had on his desk since I've known him. He gives the book an absent-minded but affectionate rub, the way you might pet a cat dozing in your lap. "I've been meaning to talk to you about something." I'm centered all of a sudden, excited. A decision has been made. "How's your new assistant working out?

He's not from Spain, right?" Tad's face is a huge, eager smile. Since taking us public and becoming a multimillionaire, Tad needs a lot of reassurance that things are good between us. He is referencing Matias, from Spain, one of Motion Innovations's first assistants, who made three thousand dollars' worth of long-distance calls home during his first, and last, month on the job.

"Oh my God. Matias. *I am so sorry. I think of it like, how you say? A leetle drop in bucket?*" I say, granting Tad what he needs by doing the Matias impression we've done for a decade. Tad presses his eyes closed with his thumb and forefinger—it looks like he has a headache, but I can hear little bursts of air coming from his nose in a near-silent laugh. When the bursts have stopped, he stays as is for a moment, in the position of a migraineur. I'm just about to ask him if everything is okay, when he rubs his eyes and slowly opens them.

"Those were the days, weren't they?" he says.

"You're telling me." It takes me a few extra seconds, but I think to say, "But look how far we've come." Tad's favorite subject is how far we've come. He flings his eyes up to the exposed air duct above his head—a quick prayer of thanks. Tad has become afraid not to say thank you for everything. I see him look up at the ceiling like this multiple times a day. Tad used to be pudgy, and greedy, and wear flannel shirts. Now he is fit and grateful, and his collar is held upright with stays and grazed by semi-long hair.

"You've got that right. We've come a long way. And so have *you.*"

A rogue beach ball from Andre's meeting bonks the glass wall. Andre jogs over to retrieve it—he's been seeing a trainer. His hair bounces up and down as he jogs back to his seat—it could definitely be tied in a ponytail. I can't decide how to respond, and I finally go with, "Haven't we all."

Tad looks pained. He inhales, holds his breath, and then lets it out in a noisy rattle. "Phaaaa," he says on the out-breath. "I need to talk to you about Baybridge. They're coming on board, no pun intended," he says, clearly nervous. "Jane, there's no easy way to say this. You worked so hard to develop that motor, but this comes from the CEO. They want Andre." Tad covers half his face with his hand—it's impossible to have a private meeting in his glass office. "I told them I respectfully disagreed, that you're the woman for the job and were responsible for every single thing they like about our motor, but they were firm. Said they like his energy, that it's in line with their target customers, Generation Z and the millennials."

"It's a fucking train door motor. The millennials aren't going to even know it's there."

"I know, believe me, I tried." Tad pauses and looks at me as if for the first time. "Are you okay?"

"I'll be fine, Tad. I've had bigger disappointments in this office."

"No, I mean . . . Never mind." He brightens suddenly and changes the subject. "Hey, what time does that thing start tonight? Sarah has told me ten times. I'm afraid to ask her again."

"Six."

"This is the girls' last holiday pageant in lower school, can you believe it?" The girls are Cate and Chloe, Tad and Sarah's twin daughters. They are ranked junior skiers, stars of the Denver Day track team, straight A students, and nice girls, too.

"No, I can't," I say. And because I know that Tad finds the passage of time a humbling and motivating force, and thus a good way to bring our conversation to an end, I add, "Time sure does fly."

Despite my disappointment, I'm able to work out a rotor tweak for the pump in our latest dialysis machine, but by 4:00 p.m., all attempts at work have been abandoned. Something bumps my chair. It's the Mighty Mobile, a robotic mail cart that eliminates the need for people to hand-deliver commonly used goods in workspaces, one of our early developments. There's a bucket on the top shelf containing invitations. *Join Tad in Conference Room A, where we will turn in our Operation 2020 Self-Inventory and Plan of Attack worksheets and toast to the new year! Hooyah!* The invite officially cuts the ribbon on the holiday break, and my colleagues begin forming a conga line of sorts. They trail between the pods toward Conference Room A, some wearing blinking Christmas-light necklaces and hats; Andre, of course, wearing an ugly Christmas sweater, a lame joke. I pull my SEALs worksheet out of my briefcase, with its one handwritten line now bisected by a faint smear of blood. From our high-rise windows, the view is dominated by clouds that sag heavy over the Mile High City, blocking the snow-covered mountains. I stuff the ruined form back into my briefcase and sneak out past Conference Room A, where champagne glasses are being raised.

IT'S DARK BY the time I reach the Denver Day School campus, so I can see that this year's tuition hike is being put to good use—tasteful white Christmas lights festoon the large old trees and the gables of the buildings, or halls, as they're called on campus. Larimer Hall of the Performing Arts glows in the distance, and those who are heading up the stone path toward its warm entrance are hurrying—the show will start soon. Vice Principal O'Malley is at the two-hundred-pound door.

"Miss Jane," he says in greeting. His back is very straight, his stomach very round, giving him the appearance of a butler. "Happy holidays. I believe Mr. Smith and his parents are saving you a seat." He guides me inside and gestures toward the back of my husband's head. If it's possible for the back of a person's head to look anxious, Allen's does. It darts side to side ever so slightly—he is following the preshow action in the wings of the stage, where occasionally a teacher or nervous student peeks out from behind the curtain. I recognize these flickering head motions. Allen is scanning for an Aiden disturbance. There's no need. It has found him.

"Allen!" Mrs. King, the first-grade teacher, says. *Come here!* her hand gesticulates. Allen sits up too quickly, startling the parents around him. He goes to see what Aiden is doing this time, leaving his coat sprawled out over our two chairs. I shimmy between the tight rows of parents, past Andre, whose son, Bradbury, is a standout first grader who wears his hair in something called a fauxhawk, a style that looks like a lawn mower accident. *It's the damnedest thing,* he told a group of us at work as he scrolled through photos documenting every angle of his child's hairstyle. *It's just who the little man wants to be.*

I settle in next to Dr. Smith, who says, "Glad you made it, Jane."

"Jane, Allen tells me that Aiden has a speaking part this year," Mrs. Smith says, glancing around the auditorium, giving it an appreciative nod. "That's very promising."

Allen exits stage left and makes his way back to our seats in a crouch—his posture a familiar one, an apology to all those around us. Allen is actually apologizing now.

"I'm sorry. I'm sorry," he says as he makes his way past the other parents, most of them my wealthy colleagues with well-behaved kids. He is too thin. He looks anemic. I met Allen near Buffalo Bill's grave on Lookout Mountain in Golden, where we'd both been hiking. Allen used to be an avid hiker. He hiked thirty-eight of Colorado's fifty-three fourteener mountains, hoping to climb them all by age forty, but he stopped when Aiden was very young. He never hikes anymore—that slow, steady climb to the top, to the vista where you get to see what lies beyond. Whenever he gets the chance, he runs for miles in flat circles around our subdivision. When I first saw him on that mountain, Allen looked so strong, like he'd grown up from the earth along with the trees that shaded the trail. I wonder, would he have followed me down it if he'd known where it would lead?

"What happened?" I ask, comforted by the immediacy of the task at hand—worrying about Aiden.

"They had to dim the lights for him, too bright. But Mrs. King said that Aiden helped Kevin tie his angel costume." I grip Allen's hand in excitement at this last bit of news.

All the lights dim now, conducting us parents into silence. The velvet curtain opens to reveal a peasant with a fauxhawk under the spotlight—and no, no, it's not my imagination—it is dyed red and green.

"Long ago, in the town of Nazareth," Bradbury begins.

The spotlight moves now on to Tad's daughter Cate, who is scrubbing a spot on the stage floor. With her corn-silk hair, white robes, and pale skin, she seems translucent, celestial.

"What can I help you with?" she asks of an angel, who explains that she will deliver the son of God. "But wait. I'm not married. I can't have a baby!" Tad is sitting in the front row, and I see his head tilt back, his eyes no doubt cast upward in thanksgiving. Joseph agrees to wed Mary, and they make their trip to Bethlehem, where they rest in a bed of barnyard straw. A chorus arranged on bleacher steps sings "What Child Is This?" in high voices as a group of shepherds makes its way onto the stage.

"Look, everyone, an angel! Not just one, many angels!"

Allen squeezes my hand tight. There's Grossman-from-Finance's son, who's chunky and wears glasses, and looks sweet in his angel costume; and Kevin, who Aiden helped; and finally, there's Aiden. His Uggs are poking out from under his robe and static has re-electrified his hair, but he is walking in a straight line, and his costume is still white. Allen and I look at each other. *See?* our eyes say. *See our precious boy.*

The spotlight moves onto Aiden. He is almost out of the woods—this is his line. He raises his arms, and for a moment the sleeves of his robe fan out as designed. Then he covers his eyes and bobs his head. Allen half sits up out of his chair, but freezes. We are practically trapped among the parents, and what is he going to do, the vacuum cleaner onstage? Aiden pulls at his collar as if he's being strangled and dances around like a bug has flown up his robe. The other kids have broken character and are staring at our son, some of them letting nervous giggles carry across the stage. Aiden finally pulls the bottom of the gown up and almost off, but it's too long and flops forward over his head. He is screaming now. Mrs. King, frightened, pulls the robe off of him, revealing our red-faced boy, singing his tortured solo, his hair sticking up all over the place. Is this just who our little man wants to be? We trip our way down the aisle. Andre has taken charge of clearing a path for us, instructing the other parents to get up and out of our way.

VICE PRESIDENT O'MALLEY holds the door to Larimer Hall open for us. As we pass over the threshold, I hear Mrs. King saying over the microphone, "Well, that was not on script." The heavy door closes on relieved laughter. Aiden reaches toward the closed door, kicking his father, who's trying hard to hold on to him.

"I want to go back," he screams. His words echo off the grand campus's stone buildings and courtyard. *Go back, back, ack.*

"You can't," Allen cries. "Goddamn it, Aiden! There are some things you do and that's it. You can't go back." *Can't go back, ack.*

"Allen, the whole school can hear you!" Mrs. Smith is loud whispering.

Dr. Smith, whose nerves have been steeled by decades of obstetric emergencies, is reading a plaque that explains the history of Larimer Hall of the Performing Arts, his hands in the pockets of his khakis. "I'm not going to keep saying this. It's time," he says, still reading, "to move on from this sensory processing nonsense and get a legitimate diagnosis from a legitimate physician, not some quack."

"We'll discuss this over dinner," Mrs. Smith says. "Allen, Jane, get him under control so we can go."

Dr. Smith finally turns away from the plaque and says, "I'm not convinced it isn't a matter of discipline. Perhaps our money would be better spent at military school."

"Dad, he's six," Allen says. To my horror, Allen begins to cry.

"Okay, Aiden, calm down for Grandmother, it's time to go to the restaurant."

"For Chrissake, Elaine," I say. "We're not going to Morton's!" *Ortons, ortons.*

DR. AND MRS. Smith escape to their rental car, and we manage to get Aiden into his booster seat in the 4Runner. Allen sits beside him in the back, trying to calm him down. It's not working. Aiden kicks the back of my seat, the thumps registering with surprising force. He is tired but relentless.

"Please! Please! Give me, Daddy. Let me try again!" Allen is holding Aiden's angel costume in his lap.

"Don't be afraid! See, Mommy? Let. Me. Try. Again!"

A blast of cold air hits when Allen rolls the window down. He lets the angel costume unfurl in the wind like a white flag of surrender before releasing it. I check the mirror and see it land in a heap of dirty snow. The sounds Aiden makes. They sink heavy into my chest. And they have me confused—I have to check the next street sign because, even on these familiar roads, for a moment I can't tell what direction we're headed in. Allen stares out the window. I'm surprised by what he's done, but I understand. Aiden will, God willing, get another shot at many things in life, but being an angel with a speaking line in the Denver Day School holiday pageant is not one of them. Sometimes you can't go back. We absorb the truth of this in the reverberations of Aiden's screams.

From six years of experience, we know that keeping a tired Aiden contained in his car seat and taking a drive is the best way to knock him out. So we drive—along I-25, which could take us on our way to the mountains if we wanted to go; past Washington Park, where we used to drink wine on lazy summer days; through Cherry Creek, where all the nice houses are; and finally, back to our house. We idle in the driveway, not able to bear waking our son. I notice that my husband has put the electric Christmas candles in our windows.

"You better turn that candle off in Aiden's room before we get upstairs," I whisper, staring into its peaceful glow.

"He's had it on all night for three nights."

"You're kidding me. You put these up three nights ago?" I hadn't noticed.

"Jane?" I can barely hear him. "I don't want to go home yet." So we don't. I drive past the Bed Bath & Beyond, past the mall to Center Point Office Park, where the Motion Innovations building is, back to the highway and off again, to the frontage road. Half of a rooster's comb glows on a neon sign. There are a couple of beat-up cars in the far corner of the lot. I pull into a space right up front.

"Are we just going to leave him here?" Allen asks.

"Why not? We'll definitely hear him if somebody tries to steal him away."

"We're terrible," Allen says.

"Come on, we'll sit in that booth right there," I say, pointing toward a frosty window. "We can see right out to the car. We'll keep an eye on him."

We are so careful not to wake our son that it takes us five full minutes to exit the car. Aiden sleeps against the booster's plush side wing, legs dangling—I resist giving him a kiss before we go.

We cover him with the wool blanket that I keep in my car in case of emergencies and close the car doors by slowly, very slowly, pressing our bodies against them to muffle the sound. He doesn't wake up. We are so excited, we swing our hands in a little dance in the parking lot, and Allen gives me a kiss in the cold, crisp air.

"We can't," he says when we break apart. "He'll freeze."

"One drink. That's my emergency blizzard blanket. The salesman at REI guaranteed warmth for six hours in freezing temperatures. Nobody will even notice." I make a sweeping gesture to encompass the mostly empty lot.

"Okay," he says. "Let's go."

The old Pizza Hut is warm. Two old-timers sit hunched over beers on either end of the bar, and Brenda, the giver of the receipt, is in the center, not near either of them, staring up at the television. Allen settles into the cracked red-vinyl booth so that he can keep an eye on Aiden while I get our drinks. Without taking her eyes off the TV, Brenda says, "My brother has taken a shine to that Cabo San Lucas, so I might be taking care of you here for a while." Oh, Jesus.

"Fantastic. In that case, I'll start with two Sunning Dogs."

She remembers my order and takes care not to pour us foamy beers. The guy next to me is my Moscow mule date, Wally, my favorite old-timer, but he doesn't seem to remember me. "That Sheila E. is one badass bitch," he's telling his friend while hand drumming on the bar.

I notice that Brenda has done something out of the ordinary; she has decorated The Rooster for Christmas. Primary-colored lights are strung across the bar, silver tinsel runs along the backs of booths. I carry the brimming pints over to our booth, slide in across from my husband. With each cold sip of beer, warmth spreads through my muscles. I hold Allen's hand across the table.

"Let's do this every night," he smiles. The beer and the warmth of the bar have brought some color back to his face. "What are we going to do with him?" he asks, dreamy, staring out the window into some middle distance.

I don't answer. Instead, I pick up the snow globe Brenda has placed in the center of our table. It looks like a crystal ball, the scene inside a family of five holding hands, ice-skating, the youngest one spinning away from the pack. I give the globe a shake. I never told anybody this, not even Allen. Everyone wondered why I insisted on naming my son Aiden, so close to Allen. It was the closest I could think of to the word Eden. That's what it felt like to me when they put him on my chest, where he fit perfectly in its deep ravine. Eden.

After threatening to all day, it begins to snow—large, white, fluffy flakes, not the slush that sometimes falls from the Colorado sky. The cozy feeling of The Rooster and watching the snow fall from behind the frosty window take me back suddenly, thirty-five years, to the back seat of my parents' car, the Wyoming landscape being blanketed by holiday snow that we would make fresh tracks on the next day when we arrived at our destination, usually Sleeping Giant Ski Resort. My mom checks on me in the rearview. I'm great. I'm handwriting my goals for the future in the fog of the cold car window—curlicues and Christmas trees, snowflakes and a stick figure in skis about to take on a mountain.

"Can you imagine the skiing tomorrow?" Allen says, admiring

the falling snow, his voice light. He, too, has been carried away. "Maybe . . ." he says, but doesn't finish the thought.

We sit in silence and drink. The snow is really coming down now. "We better get going," Allen says, his voice a minor tone.

"Time to go," I agree, but neither one of us makes a move to get up. The snow is so heavy it obscures our view of the car. You can't see two feet in front of your face in weather like this. A pair of headlights cuts through the flurry. I follow their trails of light. This reminds me—at our house, in every window, we have left the candles on.

Annie Barnett got her start writing fiction at the UCLA Extension Writers' Program and is a winner of the James Kirkwood Literary Prize. She lives in Los Angeles with her husband. "What Child Is This?" is her first published story.

Editor's Note

The first line of Jason Baum's "Rocket" commanded my attention. It had a definitive, yarn-spinning voice and cadence, held suspense, and was already mildly comical about what seemed a serious subject.

There are so many ways for a story to not quite fulfill itself, and I'm often waiting with a bit of held breath as I read a submission, hoping a story that initially compels me will be born whole. Will it keep me curious, be clear, entertaining, with issues vital enough to sustain my attention? Will it deliver a critical, plot-hinged turning point? Will the conclusion surprise yet feel inevitable?

At *Bellevue Literary Review*, we've received many submissions about addiction but few about recovery. In this tale, the narrator describes his friend T-Rex's magical realism scheme to get himself sober, relates his own addiction journey, and, in doing so, covers the whole nine yards of recovery: love, faith, shame, striving, failure, triumph. "Rocket," with its wise, desperate, knuckleheaded, struggling community of characters, is shot through with compassionate humor. One could do worse, seeking help or understanding addiction, than to start with Jason Baum's story.

Suzanne McConnell, Fiction Editor
Bellevue Literary Review

Rocket

Jason Baum

THE ONLY METH HEAD I EVER LIKED WAS THIS GUY everybody called T-Rex. We both collected old sci-fi comics and hated rehabs. He was one of the regulars at the AA Fellowship I'd been going to, who, despite his best efforts, could never string together more than a few weeks' clean. The nickname *T-Rex* wasn't because he was some ferocious carnivore or anything, it's just that his arms were abnormally thin in proportion to the rest of his bulky body, like a tyrannosaur. His real name was Kelly.

One night while I'm cleaning the Fellowship bathrooms, I overhear people asking about T-Rex. Nobody had seen him in a few weeks, which usually meant one of the three relapse inevitabilities: *in jail, in rehab,* or *dead.* That's the saying around here, whether you're a drinker or a drugger.

Then this guy who's always sleeping on the couch says it wasn't any of those things, T-Rex was just building a rocket in his backyard.

"Like a missile?" somebody asks.

"No, no. Like a ship," the guy says. "A rocket ship."

"Where's he think he's going?" another guy barks.

"T-Rex can barely read," a woman says. "How's he gonna build a rocket?"

I keep scrubbing at the grout between the sink tiles while the debate outside the bathroom carries on about what T-Rex did and didn't know about space flight.

It's hard to know what to believe around this place. Everybody's sober, but they still goof off and exaggerate in a belligerent *I'm gonna one-up you* sort of way. Instead of drinking contests, it's always *Oh, yeah, well, I drank five gallons of whiskey a day. Big deal, I shot two pounds of dope in one sitting. That's nothing, I've died and come back to life twenty-six times.* You have to investigate everything you hear if you want to get to the truth.

When I'm done with the sink tiles, I turn the hot faucet on, rinse the sponge out, then leave the water running. You have to get it scalding if you're going to make a dent in this place. *Half measures availed us nothing.* That's another one of my favorites.

They have all kinds of those sayings up on the walls. *First Things First. 24 Hours at a Time.* I take the canned recovery-isms seriously because I don't want to end up *in jail, in rehab,* or *dead.* I want the *happy, joyous, and free* that everybody else has. That saying is front and center above the Fellowship door.

When the water is hot enough to blister, I soak a Brillo pad, add some bleach, and start in on the toilets. The whole time I'm thinking about T-Rex going into space. We'd worked the steps during one of his more earnest stretches of sobriety, and I'd watched him struggle to get through one page of the Big Book. Though in hindsight, I'm wondering if maybe he'd been faking it to get out of doing the hard work. Addicts and alcoholics will pull your leg clean off if you let them. I catch myself doing it all the time.

———

A COUPLE DAYS later on Saturday, I stop by the trailer park where T-Rex lives to see for myself what he's been up to. Gathering evidence has been critical in my first year of sobriety. Seeing something with my own eyes helps me sort out what's real and what's not.

As soon as I park my car, I see the rocket. It's school bus–sized and fills the empty lot next to the trailer park. It looks like one you'd see in a 1950s B movie, with a bright-red nose cone on top, standing on four matching red fins at the bottom. The steel body has one circular window on the side. Several side panels are lying on the ground, leaving all the wires and cables poking out from the ship's insides.

I walk over to where T-Rex and this guy in a white lab coat are standing in front of the rocket and a giant whiteboard with mathematical equations scribbled on it. T-Rex is all worked up, pointing at the rocket with his wiry reptile arms and shouting about something called "the Orbital Trim Maneuver."

"You're not taking into account the speed of millimeters versus meters per second," T-Rex is insisting.

The guy in the lab coat throws his arms up in frustration. "It's mass and propellant, *mass and propellant!*"

I wonder if T-Rex is clean. With meth heads, it's hard to tell. Looking at his weathered, pockmarked face, you'd guess he's in his late fifties, but I know he's somewhere in his midthirties like me. Plus, meth does a number on the central nervous system, and none of the telltale spasms ever go away. T-Rex's little arms always twitch like he's about to punch you, and he makes this weird clicking noise with his tongue. Sometimes his eyes will do this violent blink like the lids are being yanked down over and over.

Every time I'm around T-Rex, I'm reminded of how the doctor

told me they can only draw blood from my left arm. All the years of shooting junk and Oxy left the veins in my right arm shot to hell forever. He actually used the word *forever*.

Finally, T-Rex stops midsentence and turns to me with a grin, his tongue clicking. "Hey, man, how's it going?"

"Just stopping by," I tell him. "Hadn't seen you around."

"I know, I know," he says apologetically. "I'm working on something."

I whistle in awe at the rocket. "Sure is pretty. Where'd you get it?"

"I know a guy," T-Rex says, which is believable, considering the resourcefulness of meth heads. There is nothing in the world they can't find, and even if they couldn't they'd know somebody who could.

"Where are you going?" I ask.

"Nowhere, really," he says. "I'm just gonna drift in orbit for a year or so and get some real clean time."

"I'm the last fucking person to say this, but can't you just go back to rehab?" I ask, wondering what would happen if T-Rex put a fraction of this effort into working his steps.

"Rehab's not enough," T-Rex says. "I've been to eleven, and it's the same thing every fucking time. Two weeks in—and then I'm out. The doors aren't locked, you know?"

"*The doors aren't locked.*" Another well-known Fellowship saying. I think of my own multiple rehabs, and how easy it is to vacate the premises when the doors aren't locked.

T-Rex looks up to the sky and raises a tiny hand to shade his eyes from the sun. "I'll have no choice but to sit tight and let the days add up," he says. "Then I'll come back, walk right into the Fellowship, and get my one-year chip."

"When do you leave?"

"In a week. Next Thursday."

"Next *Friday*," the man in the white lab coat counters. "Better weather."

"Next Thursday *or* Friday." T-Rex nods to the man in the lab coat. "This is Ken, by the way. He's my engineer." Ken smiles politely.

"How are you gonna land?" I ask.

"I've got an old parachute," T-Rex says.

"With a hole in it," Ken adds.

"We'll patch it up in time for launch," T-Rex says confidently.

"Patch it up?" I ask.

"Yeah, check these babies out." T-Rex snaps the waistband of his shorts. "I got a connect who's giving me a thousand of these nylon swim trunks we can use. It'll be like new."

I try to hide my growing skepticism as I glance between Ken, the rocket, and the barely legible whiteboard. T-Rex must sense my lack of faith, because he assures me there's no cause for alarm. "You know those visors on the space helmets," he says, flipping his little hand in front of his face. "The things that go up and down for the sun?"

"Yeah."

"Ken's uncle invented those. So, all of this is a piece of cake." They segue into a discussion about jet propulsion and centripetal acceleration. I try to follow along but get lost when they veer into linear algebra.

I hear a door slam and see T-Rex's mom coming out of the trailer toward us, carrying his beagle, Dougie. She was usually happy to see me when I picked up T-Rex for step work, but now she doesn't say hi or anything. She just drops the dog to the ground and walks away. I do a double take when I see the dog is missing its left front leg. The tripod-angular way it's hobbling toward us reminds me of wounded soldiers crawling across a battlefield in an old war movie.

T-Rex jogs over to the dog, picks it up, and nuzzles its face. Then he rejoins Ken and their conversation about astronomical twilight, and the way the sun will reflect off the fuselage and keep him warm when he leaves the upper atmosphere.

I DO A lot more than clean the bathrooms at the Fellowship. Monday through Friday, I arrive at 7:00 p.m. sharp, dressed in slacks and a button-up, shake hands with people at the front door and hand out books before the meetings, pour coffee if needed. Afterward, I collect all the books and stack them neatly on the shelves, then deal with the bathroom and make sure I'm back to the SLE, my "Sober Living Environment," in time for curfew.

Tonight, Monday night, I'm scrubbing the walls in the bathroom with the door propped open so I can listen to the post-meeting gossip in the other room. Who's got the most clean time and who's sleeping with whom this week. They're calling tomorrow's 10:00 p.m. meeting *the Meat Market* from all the hooking up that goes on. When the chatter turns to T-Rex's trip to outer space, opinions vary from aggression to disbelief.

"He's gonna blow his damn self up," one man says. "*Kablooey!*"

"Why can't he just come to meetings like the rest of us?" one guy grumbles.

"Maybe it'll work," a woman says. "I knew an alcoholic Navy SEAL who sat at the bottom of the ocean for six months. Came back up and never touched another drop of booze."

"T-Rex never found *God*," one guy finally declares. "That's what his problem is."

God. God's a funny thing around this place. It's always God this and God that. *God, God, God, God, God*. Everybody swears that God is the key to staying sober. In fact, God's the whole reason I'm scouring the bathroom every night.

A couple months ago, I was staring at one of the sayings on the walls, *Let Go and Let God*, when one of the old-timers, Eddie, said to me, "That's the truth right there."

"I don't have any evidence of God," I told him.

Eddie looked at me, jaw-dropped and wide-eyed. With forty years under his belt, he's been sober longer than he was drinking. "How much time do you have?" he asked.

"Almost a year."

"What's tripping you up?"

"I guess I can't figure out the difference between God and the people who believe in God."

"Ah, that old chestnut," Eddie said. "Well, a year in the rooms isn't *that* long. You better find your God or else it's *in jail, in rehab*, or *dead*."

"Well, I don't want those." I'd had plenty of the first two, and pretty sure I encountered the third, either that or it was just strong dope. Still, When you're blessed with the gift of desperation, you'll try anything. "All right, Eddie, enlighten me—how do I find God?"

"You could start by cleaning the bathroom," Eddie said. "Everybody finds God in there."

"Bullshit."

"No bullshit," he said. "That's where I found him."

At first, I wondered if the old-timer was setting me up for some kind of prank, on account of how funny everybody here thinks they are. But at some point, I'd gotten obedient and just started saying yes to everything people told me to do. Pour coffee during the meetings. *Okay.* Raise your hand and introduce yourself as an addict or alcoholic. *Sure thing.* When somebody has what you want, you do what they do, and these people have what I want: the cars, the dates, the families. All the *happy, joyous, and free* stuff.

Sinks are the easiest. I'm scrubbing those down fast now. I even started using an old toothbrush under the lip of the toilet bowl. The Brillo pad was good, but the toothbrush has a better angle and gets the grime a Brillo can't reach. I'll use the toothbrush five minutes clockwise, five counterclockwise.

When I'm finished, I stare at the bits of black and green crud resting in the base of the toilet bowl. I'm getting pretty good at this. I flush it down, turn on the hot faucet, and go to the hall closet to get the mop, bucket, and Pine-Sol. Twenty minutes mopping the floor and I'll be done.

Afterward, the bathrooms practically glisten. They look better than they ever have. But two months of thorough cleaning and I'm still not feeling any connection to God, a Higher Power, the universe, or whatever you want to call it. No burning bushes in the stalls, no blinding lights from the faucet. I think it's a pretty dick move on God's part to see me doing all this hard work and not even pop in to say hello.

WEDNESDAY BEFORE THE launch, T-Rex calls and asks if I can give him a ride to Modesto to pick up a few things for his space trip. *Methdesto* is what the tweakers call the town. T-Rex says a guy there owes him money for an old meth deal, but instead of money he's going to give him the swim trunks for the parachute, and a few pallets of

Aquafina water, beef jerky, and expired graham crackers. I told him sure, and I'd get somebody to cover my Fellowship chores as long as there was no meth involved. He asked if he could bring his dog along.

It's a hot night. The air feels warm blowing on our faces. For some reason, once I got sober, long stretches of driving became fun, though normally I can't sit still. On the weekends, I drive to different fellowships up and down the coast where nobody knows me. It's a different kind of anonymity.

T-Rex is holding Dougie on his lap, rubbing the nub where the dog's leg used to be. He asks if he can put the radio to a country station, which I can't stand, but the guy is going into space for a year, so I let him. Who knows what kind of reception he'll be able to get up there.

"What made you think of going to outer space?" I ask him.

T-Rex twitchy-shifts the beagle, reaches into his pocket, and pulls out a crumpled piece of paper. "I found this line in the Big Book," he says, tongue clicking. Then he reads, *"We have found much of heaven and we have been rocketed into a fourth dimension of existence of which we had not even dreamed."*

"I knew you could read," I tell him, and he laughs.

"I want that other existence," T-Rex says. "I'm tired of this one. All hooked on meth. Can't do shit right. My mom won't even look at me. Up there I can stay focused. No more bullshit."

"Otherwise it's *in jail, in rehab*, or *dead*," I say.

"In jail, in rehab, or *dead*," T-Rex repeats, his tongue clicking like a lighter. "You'll see, I'm gonna get in that fourth dimension with the rest of you."

"I don't think I'm there yet," I tell him.

"Horseshit," he says. "You're staying clean, you almost got a year."

"A year isn't *that* long."

"It's a strong fucking start," he says. "And you got the job, the family, all of it."

"Dude, I fill sample bottles of high-end lotion," I tell him.

"It's still a job."

"And my mom only talks to me once a month. Last time it was three and a half minutes."

"At least she's talking to you," he says.

We hit a stretch of empty highway that opens up the sky. Billions of stars turn on in an instant. I check my speed limit and eye my rearview for cops. Those instincts never really go away.

T-Rex points one of his tyrannosaur arms out the window. "If you get a telescope, you'll be able to see me once a month. Ken's got walkie-talkies, so I'll be able to talk to you guys when I'm in line with the TV satellite on my mom's trailer."

I notice his other hand never leaves the dog's stump. "What happened to Dougie?" I ask.

T-Rex rubs the dog's ears and kisses its forehead, his arms twitching. He moves a clenched fist against his chest like he wants to hit himself. His whole face scrunches, then he pounds his fist on the side of his head like he's trying to knock water out of his ear. "I don't know what happened. I was cooking a batch of shit, same shit I cooked a million times. It only blew off Dougie's paw, but the vet said it was safer to take the whole leg."

"Jesus fucking Christ." I wince, then realize he's already beaten himself into the ground over it. "Sorry, man." The dog shifts on T-Rex's lap. It looks like it wants to scratch behind its ear with the phantom leg but gets confused when there's no limb to use. T-Rex scratches his ear for him.

"Wait—where are you getting the fuel for the rocket?" I ask.

"Me and Ken are cooking it up," he says. "Before you say any-thing, just know that meth is more combustible than jet fuel. I can do jet fuel in my sleep."

"If you say so."

"I'm telling you," T-Rex says, his tongue loudly clicking. "I'll be a new person when I get back. Just like you and everybody else at the Fellowship. I'll get a job and go on dates and all that other stuff. I'll even buy my mom a new house. A nice clean one."

"*A nice clean one*," I repeat, not meaning to.

We pass a sign that says Modesto is twenty miles away. T-Rex says our exit will be the third one. *Methdesto*, he whispers, then asks if it's okay to smoke a cigarette in the car. He's not going to be able to smoke for the next year, so I figure what the hell.

"I've been cleaning the Fellowship bathrooms," I tell him. "One of the old-timers says I'll find God in there."

"I heard that one before," T-Rex says, nodding.

"And?"

"I never tried it, but maybe you'll have some luck," he says, then looks out the window. "I think maybe I'll meet God up there."

"What are you gonna say to him?"

"Not sure," T-Rex says and takes a long drag. "I packed a nice suit, though. Figure I should look good for the occasion. What are you gonna say to God if you find him in the bathroom?"

I think about all the routines I have in place. I'd heard one of the old-timers say active addiction is mass chaos, so our sobriety needs to be rigidly organized, like tasks to cross off a list.

Wake up early, go to work. Get off work and go back to the SLE. Change into slacks and a button-up for the AA meeting.

Get to the Fellowship by 7:00 p.m. *sharp*. Hand out books. Make and pour coffee. Raise my hand and share during the meeting. Clean the bathrooms, starting at the top of the walls. Hit the sinks and toilets with sponges, toothbrushes, scalding-hot water, soap, and bleach. Mop until the room smells of pure Pine-Sol. Repeat the routine five days a week. Otherwise, it's *in jail, in rehab*, or *dead.*

"I'm gonna tell God I'm fucking tired," I say. "I'm tired and I don't have much energy left."

T-Rex is nodding, his tongue clicking like a light switch. He blows smoke rings out the window. "I think your nickname should be Mr. Clean," he says. "Like the guy from the commercials."

"That works," I tell him. "Mr. Clean like the guy from the commercials *and* Mr. Clean because I'm clean and sober."

"Also, you look like Mr. Clean from the commercials, 'cuz you're going bald, you know?"

"*What?*"

"Yeah, man, your hair is super thin. Why don't you just shave it? It'll look better."

"Fuck you, man, I just have thin hair!"

"Don't be so sensitive." T-Rex laughs. "Embrace that shit."

T-Rex pretends to scrub the dashboard with his tyrannosaur hands like he's scrubbing toilets, then he roars like the king of the lizards. Dougie's head perks up. We laugh and turn the music up, the stars above us illuminating the deserted highway. T-Rex leans his head out the window into the hot wind, like he's absorbing all the warmth he can while he's here on the earthly plane.

———

THE NEXT NIGHT, I'm sitting in a meeting, eyeballing this guy in the back of the room who calls himself Homeless Carl. He's another regular at the Fellowship, not because he comes here to get sober, but because he comes to eat the food, drink the coffee, and use the bathroom as a shower.

Usually, I'm able to beat him into the bathrooms and lock the doors, because if I don't, it's big fucking trouble. I'll have to wait an hour for him to get out, then at least thirty minutes to air the place out. I can't even describe the smell he leaves lingering behind. Unfortunately, it's a smell I know intimately from my own time living on the streets. Like T-Rex, the guy reminds me of things I'd rather forget, especially that.

One night I asked Eddie if there was anything I could do to keep Homeless Carl from using the bathrooms. "Can't we tell him to go to a YMCA or something?"

"Nope," Eddie said, then tapped one of the sayings on the wall: *Some of us are sicker than others.* As soon as the meeting ends, Homeless Carl stands and wheels his tattered travel suitcases with him into the bathroom, sealing my fate for the evening. I stay seated, envisioning what I'd be doing in there if he wasn't in my way. Wiping walls, sinks, tiles. Tonight I've got to get around the little metal nuts that bolt the toilets to the floor. I forgot to get those last time.

All around me people are filing out of the meeting room and into the kitchen for post-meeting gossip and coffee. I should start collecting books but I'm stuck in a trance, fuming over the damage being done to *my* bathrooms.

I snap out of it when a guy comes up to me, hands me a couple of books, smiles, and says, "Here you *God.*"

Another guy gives me two more books, saying cheerfully, "What a *God* meeting, don't you think?"

Then a lady adds three more to the growing pile on my lap and winks. "Have a *God* night."

"Ha ha, very funny," I snap as they walk away. "I know what you guys are doing." I gather the rest of the books and stack them on the bookcase in sharp, upright rows, when I hear the chatter around the Fellowship beginning to morph and meld into a God-soaked nightmare. God is the only word on everyone's lips.

"God, *God*?" I hear somebody ask.

"God," a man replies.

"God, God *God*," a woman cackles.

And then it's everywhere. I grab the trash in the kitchen and everybody's buzzing with *God, God, God, God, God*. Outside, when I dump the trash in the bin, everybody on the patio is *God, God, God, God, God*. By the time I'm back inside the Fellowship, Homeless Carl is leaving the bathroom and I jump in and lock the door behind me, panting, hearing echoes of *God, God, God* and inhaling the foul smell in the air. I gag, then hold my breath, unbutton my shirt, and wrap it around my face.

I pick up the gloves and cleaning products from beneath the sink and try to power through, starting at the top of the walls and working my way down, but no matter how hard I scrub or breathe through my mouth, I keep gagging.

I tighten the shirt around my face and half finish wiping down the sinks. It smells so bad that I want to cry, but instead I start to laugh. The more I laugh the more the smell gets in. I'm laughing and gagging, laughing and gagging. Every time I laugh the smells punch through the shirt into my face. The smells of an unbathed body, unbrushed teeth, excrement. All in my mouth and nose and lungs. I feel a small jolt in my chest, and more phlegm shifts. I suddenly remember this time my mom brought me a sandwich and a change of clothes when I was sleeping in the park and the way she kept all the windows rolled down in the car while we talked.

I crash into the stall, take the shirt off my face, and puke all over the toilet and onto the floor. It smells even worse here. I laugh and puke again. Then I'm just kneeling in front of the toilet, puking and laughing. I've heard the old-timers say that God has an odd sense of humor, and maybe this is my first glimpse of it.

When it's all out of my system, I pull myself up to the sink, wash the front of my shirt, and splash cold water on my face.

THE MORNING OF the launch, I drive to T-Rex's trailer park to see him off. There's a circle of barricade bars around the rocket and a couple dozen people gathered in the lot. Ken is wheeling a ladder in front of the ship and checking items on a clipboard in his hands. I'm going to be late for work, but I think it'll be worth it. There's only so many chances you get to see something like this.

I make my way through the crowd toward a few people I recognize from the Fellowship. As usual, they're hemming and hawing about the events unfolding.

"T-Rex better bring a jacket," one guy grunts. "That's all he needs is to catch a damn cold up there."

"Think he'll make it?" one woman asks.

"Not a chance," one guy says. "It's about to be *kablooey*."

"I dunno," one guy says. "He just might make it."

"He'll make it if he finds that fourth dimension," I say. They all nod in agreement.

T-Rex comes out of his trailer in full puffy space suit, glass fishtank helmet in his hands. He makes his way toward us, beaming, taking his time and waving at everybody like the astronauts do in the movies. For a moment I don't want him to go. I want him to stay here so we can keep goofing off. I hope he doesn't change too much up there in outer space. I hope when he gets back from reaching the fourth dimension we can still have fun together.

He stops at the barricade in front of his mother. She's holding Dougie in her arms but still not looking at T-Rex. I know that look she's not giving him. I know it all too well. T-Rex kisses the dog on the forehead and rubs its stump. He gives his mother a hug and speaks into her ear. I can't hear what he's telling her, but I know what he's saying: *This time will be different, I promise.* I wonder if I tell my mom about T-Rex's rocket, if maybe I can keep her on the phone for at least five minutes next time. Maybe even longer.

T-Rex climbs up the ladder, then stops and turns to wave good-bye. He smiles a gigantic meth head of a smile, missing teeth and all. We lock eyes and he firmly salutes at me, and I salute back out of re-flex. I don't think he was in the military or anything, though it never occurred to me to ask. I have to start asking people at the Fellowship about those kinds of things. Who a person used to be and who they are today. I'm sure that would be good evidence to gather. Probably has something to do with their *happy, joyous, and free.*

T-Rex climbs through the rocket window and closes it behind him. Ken passes out earplugs, then stands back with the rest of us and shouts for everybody to join him in the countdown. *Ten, nine, eight, seven, six . . .*

The rocket starts to shake. Smoke billows from between the red fins at the base.

Five!

I feel burning heat from the thrusters stretch across the lot and over my face. Gravel tumbles all around my feet, pebbles bumping up against my shoes.

Four!

Something small moves in my chest. Something really small. Smaller than a sliver stuck inside another sliver. It's right in the center of my chest by that thing that breaks when someone gives you the Heimlich maneuver.

Three!

All of a sudden, T-Rex's mother starts waving to the ship and shouting, "*That's my son, that's my son!*" and I can't wait to tell him that on the walkie-talkie. I bet it'll help him stay warm up there.

Two!

I hear the ignition and the blasting combustion of rocket fuel. A sonic boom shifts the earth.

One!

A brilliant light washes over us. I cover my eyes. The air tastes like metal and fire. I peek between my fingers and watch the rocket lift off and shoot into the sky. A corkscrew plume of smoke trailing behind it spirals up, up, and out of the atmosphere.

Jason Baum was born and raised in the East Bay. In 2024, he was awarded the PEN/Robert J. Dau Short Story Prize for Emerging Writers and participated in the Bread Loaf Writers' Conference. His fiction has been featured in *Bellevue Literary Review* and long-listed for *The Masters Review*'s 2022–23 Winter Short Story Award for New Writers. He is currently working on his debut novel-in-stories.

Editor's Note

It's axiomatic—and also universally true, in my experience—that journal editors take special pleasure in reading exciting work from hitherto-unpublished writers. Alex Boeden's odd, remarkable "Alfhild" belongs to what may be the rarest subclass of such stories. It attends no school, works from no familiar model. There are several big plot points . . . but Boeden, in what my students would call a boss move, has them take place off the page, almost in passing. It's a father-daughter tale, yes, but one that dispenses with almost every convention of the genre. "Alfhild" is so rich, so assured, and so wonderfully peculiar that I could scarcely believe it when, after the acceptance, we belatedly discovered that it was Boeden's debut.

Michael Griffith, Fiction Editor
The Cincinnati Review

Alfhild

Alex Boeden

IF HER HEAD GETS COLD, IT STARTS TO HURT, SO ON days when the sun cannot dry her hair on the short walk from the sea to Grandma's house, Alfhild's father massages her scalp until her thin, little body stops shivering under the towel. It has become a routine, a ritual almost: Alfhild finishing her late-afternoon swim with a cup of hot chocolate and her father's warm hands on her head. She stands in the kitchen with her back toward him, the cup of hot chocolate close to her chest, her head slightly bowed, her prescription swim goggles fogging in the rising column of steam.

There is, at these moments, something undeniably otherworldly about her: silent and shaking with cold like a delicate sea creature dripping on a linoleum floor, a petite and taciturn mermaid, doing her best to adapt to life on dry land. The act of massaging her scalp is, to Alfhild's father, a way to ease the transition. If he finds a ribbon of seaweed in her hair, he plucks it out and shows it to her as if to say: *Look, this is no longer part of you. The sea has let go, you are free to be human again.* Sometimes, just to upset her expressionless face, he pretends to pluck other, far more improbable things from her hair: an amber-colored pebble, a chewing-gum wrapper, a coin, a car key, a stainless-steel wristwatch. She looks on in absolute silence, and when his performance comes to an end, she puts the cup down and looks him straight in the eye, holding his gaze for a couple of seconds. Then, with a long exhalation of breath, she claps very slowly.

It is hard not to smile when he sees her like that, ironically clapping while shaking with cold, her goggles still foggy, her pale little face upturned and unsmiling. *If it makes her engage, it is good*, he argues when his wife, Clara, tells him to stop encouraging this type of behavior. He knows it is strange—unnatural, even: a five-year-old girl expressing herself with the undisguised contempt of a teen. Yet the gesture is so perfectly executed, so expertly hurtful, that to see it only in terms of antisocial behavior is to miss something that, to Alfhild's father, feels almost miraculous.

Intellectually, Alfhild is a precocious child. She passed the admission test for Mathildeskolen's preschool program in Ebeltoft with a comfortable margin. She reads at a seventh-grade level, and her active vocabulary would put most adolescents to shame. Still, her program instructors report increasingly withdrawn and aggressive behavior, and one day in March the school psychologist calls. It hits his wife hard, on their way home from Ebeltoft. Clara just sits in the passenger seat with a blank look on her face, mumbling to herself, again and again: *It's not fair, first her eyes and now this, it's not fair.* They go to a specialist in Aarhus, who interviews Alfhild and comes to the same conclusion as the school psychologist. The next doctor they see thinks it's too soon for a conclusive diagnosis, and for a while they allow themselves to believe that Alfhild is simply going through a phase. After a couple of months, however, with no noticeable change in Alfhild's behavior, they go back to the doctor and insist on having a genetic test done.

Several abnormalities are found in Alfhild's genes: presence of PVOX and ZALC3F, mutations in the region involved in Götzman-Carr and Tyro syndromes—confirmed by DNA sequencing of the IRNI2 gene, popularly known as the irony gene. The name is unfortunate, the doctor explains, since fewer than 5 percent of cases stem from mutations in this particular gene. And once more, the doctor reminds them that an accurate diagnosis requires close observation over a number of years and that frequent irony use in early childhood is not necessarily a predictor of adolescent or adult-onset PIPRAD (Pervasive Ironic Pattern Recognition and Appreciation Disorder). In fact, a former patient of his has scored even higher than Alfhild on the Williamson childhood-sarcasm scale; she is now in her twenties, still high functioning with minimal medication and no history of concomitant depression or self-destructive behavior. It's not the end of the world, the doctor assures them, most conditions can be managed; with an attentive support network, even expressive sarcastics can go on to lead long and, for all intents and purposes, happy lives.

During the following days, Alfhild's father disappears into a hole of obsessive internet research. He climbs out, pale and unshaven, clutching two facts about the disorder. Fact number one: for those who perceive it to its fullest degree, irony is one of the most exquisite patterns in nature. Fact number two: experienced irony must be expressed. According to a recent Scandinavian study, low communicative output lies at the root of all registered cases of PIPRAD-related self-mutilation. If irony is not continually conveyed, it will build up in the sufferer's mind and eventually trigger a self-harming event. As parents, the best thing they can do for their daughter is to activate her—that is, create an engaging, target-rich environment and encourage every act of expressivity, no matter how hurtful or cruel.

Clara disagrees. The angry specks of red in her cheeks have already spread to the sides of her neck, and she refuses to meet his eyes when she speaks: *You'll make it worse; if you indulge her, you'll turn her into a monster.*

He tries to explain that maybe with time and the right medication, Alfhild's output might be controlled, but right now their first priority is to point the edged blades in Alfhild's mind away from herself. In the online forums, it's often referred to as *hugging the razor*: the act of draining a loved one's irony buildup by turning yourself into a target. It's a demanding procedure. You have to lower your guard and just stand there and take it, arms by your side, letting each cutting insight land unimpeded. For Clara, it's too much to take in. He looks at her face and chooses not to insist. Together they interview several certified PIPRAD therapists in the Djursland area, and Clara decides on a young psychologist in Ålsø who treats all her patients outdoors, sitting cross-legged on a porch in front of a garden of wave-patterned gravel and a small rocky island with a miniature tree.

On the gravel, next to a flat moss-covered stone representing a turtle swimming upstream, lies a single rust-colored leaf. Alfhild's father gestures toward it. *Go on, Affi-Bee*, he whispers as Alfhild stomps through the ripple-shaped pebble formations and kicks the upstream turtle into a low bamboo fence. This is the process: once she has expressed her frustration—disrupted the garden's symmetrical patterns by upending a rock or writing something obscene in the gravel—she is given a rake and asked to restore the illusion of water. The psychologist shows her how to make pebbles into ripples and waves, and Alfhild watches with what appears to be genuine interest.

Clara is elated. *Look at her face*, she whispers, nudging him with her elbow. *Isn't it priceless? She looks so serene.* He takes his wife's hand and squeezes. *So serene*, she whispers again.

After only a month of rock-garden therapy, Clara tells him she wants a fresh start for Alfhild. She has found a school here in Grenaa, a small public school with an inclusive environment—no stigmatizing special-needs classes, no PIPRAD response plans, no irony de-escalation schemes. *She won't be popular, I know, but sooner or later she'll connect with someone.* He worries about Alfhild being bullied by classmates, but Clara insists: *She'll make a connection; you've seen how she's grown.*

Above her red backpack, her ponytail curves like a comma. He watches her go, first from the gate and then—to conceal his post-drop-off lingering—from the car or the other side of the street. If he doesn't see her enter the building, if she disappears behind the ladybug playhouse or just melts into the crowd of child-shaped blobs that amass by the sandbox, he worries. He imagines the worst, and when one day she comes to the gate—a teacher by her side, a bright-purple bruise on her forehead—he immediately starts looking for suspects, scanning each little face in the crowd for indications of guilt and poor moral fiber.

No, nobody pushed her, the teacher insists. *She got up on her own and just continued like nothing had happened, isn't that right, Alfhild?*

In the car he hears himself ask: *You know how to deal with a bully, don't you, Affi-Bee?* He tells her to look for a weakness and use it. Lisps. Freckles. Receding chins. Personal tragedy. Nothing is off-limits. She looks at him uncertainly, wincing a little as he touches her forehead.

When she falls again a few months later, Clara takes her to

an ophthalmologist who gives her a pair of bifocals and some atropine eye drops to relax her good eye. This, according to Clara, will improve her depth perception and stop her from falling and bumping into things. Alfhild hates the new glasses. On weekends at Grandma's, when they come back from the beach, Alfhild keeps her prescription swim goggles on for as long as she can. Like a little explorer from the deep blue sea, she sits at the table and stares at her food, her goggles so close to the bowl that the tips of her bangs dip into the soup. Clara gets up. *But I'm a seahorse*, Alfhild protests, squirming in her chair as her forehead is testily dabbed with a napkin.

Grandma leans forward. *Sweetie*, she says, making eye contact across the table, *seahorses use their mouths to eat.*

Alfhild stops moving. *No, Grandma.* Her voice is low but assertive. *A seahorse eats with its hair, just like a jellyfish.*

Grandma's face tightens into a puzzled expression. He tries to explain: *She's right, Mom, a seahorse's mouth is vestigial. They stun and digest their prey with the long gastric filaments growing out of their backs.*

She nods in her who-would-have-thought-it kind of way, and Alfhild adds: *A seahorse filament can eat through a clamshell and damage the bottom of a small wooden boat.*

This is their ritual, their father-daughter routine: make Grandma believe something odd and amusing and completely made-up. It's a collaborative effort, both of them adding to each other's statements, neatly arranging their made-up facts into a tall and teetering structure, building it higher and higher until either it collapses on its own or Clara intervenes, toppling their little cathedral of lies with a simple statement of fact: *No, Lily, the gravitational pull of the moon does not cause iron to accumulate in the brain—no, Lily, the front porch is not speaking to the trees in the garden through fungal networks—and no, Lily, seahorses do not sink ships in the Kattegat Sea.*

His mother's reaction is always the same: hand-over-mouth surprise followed by a laugh at her own gullibility. She looks at them both, smiling and shaking her head, then she turns to Clara and touches her arm: *Thank you, honey. I'm so glad you're on my side. Just look at those two, can you imagine what they would get up to if you weren't here?*

SOMETIME AFTER HER eleventh birthday, Alfhild starts to withdraw from the world. She loses interest in classmates and stops interacting with neighborhood children. Even so, the doctor is hesitant to discuss medication, advising them instead to focus on eye-contact exercises and active-listening training, since when PIPRAD progresses, interpersonal skills tend to decline. They continue the training. They role-play schoolyard and birthday-party scenarios. They schedule peer interactions every weekend. And still, in spite of these efforts, Alfhild makes no real attempt to connect. In desperation, Alfhild's father tries to provoke her. He engages the razor-edged blades in her mind, and with dad jokes and close-up conjuring tricks, he invites her to use them on him.

At first, he gets only eye rolls and a few cutting remarks, but from there it develops into sustained tirades and cathartic eruptions of finely honed insults. It becomes a routine, a ritual almost. In the car every morning, he takes her abuse, absorbs it in silence as he stares at the road. To show he is listening, he nods every now and again and winces a little whenever she says something truly upsetting. Outside the school, he turns off the engine and waits for his daughter to finish her diatribe. This is the challenge: to contain the emotional outpour, to keep it within the private space of the car. He gives her the time she needs to conclude, and if someone walks by and looks into the car, he returns the stare, half smiling and shrugging as if to say: *Hey, what can you do? It's just one of those days.*

One late afternoon when he comes home from work, Clara is waiting for him in the driveway. *The school called earlier today.* As she closes her eyes and exhales, he senses something rigid and sharp being stretched to its limit, a tiny steel wire singing with tension. *They didn't tell me who, but some boy, some older boy, was picking on Alfhild.* She pauses, waits for a reaction, and adds: *I know the other kid started it, but once Alfhild got going . . .* Her voice trails off, and in his mind, Alfhild's father pictures the would-be bully on the floor, hands clasped around his knees, silently rocking back and forth. *They had to call his parents to come pick him up.* He makes a sound with his nose—half snorting laugh, half sigh of relief—then he feels Clara's stare and closes his eyes and clears his throat and tries to look open to whatever she might suggest next.

Other episodes follow. A series of dumb kids at school think they can pick on his daughter, and invariably end up setting her off. In the aftermath of each incident, he is quick to express his concern for the other, the instigator, the aggressor, acknowledging the overwhelming effect of Alfhild's words: *It's a terrible thing to say, of course, but Alfhild has been bullied before, and she sometimes overreacts when she's feeling threatened or being provoked.* It works for a while. The principal sympathizes with their situation, and she does what she can to smooth things over. But one morning in class, seemingly without any provocation at all, Alfhild attacks her math teacher, Mrs. Jespersen, describing her face as a Group 1 carcinogen—that is, a substance or circumstance not just suspected but known to cause cancer in humans. It is cruel, even for Alfhild, especially given the recent bereavement suffered by Mrs. Jespersen. Still, in the principal's office, he hears himself say: *My mother's sick, she's been sick for some time, and I think Alfhild is still trying to process that.* There is a moment of silence. Clara takes out her phone and stabs at the screen with her finger.

The principal looks at them both: *As you know, I think the world of your daughter.* She grabs a box of tissues and offers it to Clara. *I know there's no malice in her, but Alfhild needs a specialized environment, and we simply don't have the resources or the required expertise.* She pauses and adds: *I'm sorry about your mother.*

They find a new school, and as soon as Alfhild has settled into her new routines, Clara moves out. They commit to maintaining a shared diagnostic log and immediately notifying each other about any upcoming change that might affect Alfhild. For months, during the drop-off debriefs, he conscientiously updates Clara on everything that is going on in his life. She, however, gives him no information at all, until she casually mentions that her new boyfriend, Bo, a much younger man, is not only living with her but also interacting with Alfhild on a regular basis: *And he's teaching her to meditate, every day after school. I've never seen her so dedicated.*

He clings to his anger, his indignation over the clear breach of protocol and the rash decision to expose their daughter to a new, significant stressor. Also, he wonders why Alfhild never said anything about a new boyfriend moving in.

Oh, it's not really meditation, Dad, she explains when he builds up the courage to ask her. *It's just breathing exercises and saying out loud that you're grateful for things, Bo's not . . .* She pauses, looks up from her book, and exhales. *Bo wears his hair in a ponytail and practices spinning back kicks in front of a mirror.* She holds his gaze for a moment and then starts piling it on, riffing on Bo's general ignorance, Bo's functional illiteracy, Bo's nunchuck collection, while he, with a look of absolute seriousness, eggs her on with nods and clarifying questions. At breakfast the next morning, he asks her if it's true that Bo never graduated high school. It is crude. He hears it himself, now that the question hangs in the air. He expects an eye roll, a snort followed by silence, but to his surprise, Alfhild nods and begins to work with his prompt. It becomes a routine, a recurring game of invention: Alfhild extemporizing between sips of tea, gradually turning the small, flat stone of his question into a temple of multiple tiers, a golden pagoda of playful disdain. He is grateful but also aware of the danger; he knows that once she goes back to her mother, all it will take is one opportune moment, one irresistibly ironic alignment of attitude or behavior, and she will tell.

The scene is easy to picture: Bo strutting into the living room, full of cosmic benevolence from having just meditated, interrupting Clara as she tries to vent her frustrations with her unreasonable ex: *Breathe, honey, slow down, don't be so hard on him, he's hurting now, yes, but he's doing his best, he's a good man, everything taken into account, a good father too.* This is the point, he imagines, where Alfhild will put her book down and tell them about the Bo-themed game that she and her dad play every morning. He pictures Clara, fingertips pressed against her forehead, a profusion of red, furious specks cascading down the sides of her neck.

Then his phone rings. Usually Clara never calls him at work, so he assumes there will be urgent, open hostility—perhaps even shouting. He lowers the volume and takes the call.

There is a rasp of static and a sound of boots on pavement, sharp clicks on the verge of breaking into a run. Her voice comes through the crackle: *Is she with you?* He answers, *No*, and adds somewhat forlornly: *This week is your week.* He is moving now, past the cubicles and the printer room.

The school is still looking—most likely Alfhild is no longer there, but the school is still looking.

They hang up before he gets to the car. This is the plan: Bo and Clara will cover every street between her house and the school; he will drive home, then check the beach and his mother's house. Five or six times, he tries Alfhild's number. By a large rock in the sand, he finds her red jacket folded into a square. He sees something in the waves and sets off at a run. He is slowed by the drag of the water. He is no longer sure what he saw. The sea is opaque, and after a few explorative sweeps with his arms, he is trembling with cold.

Are you okay? A woman in a parka is waving to him from the beach. *Do you need help?*

He is not sure what to say, so as he comes out of the water, he just smiles and moves past her, shaking his head as though she were trying to pass him a flyer or hand him a pen to sign a petition.

Do you want me to call somebody? Are you sure you're okay?

The house appears at the end of the path. His trot slows to a walk. The front door is unlocked, and in the kitchen, he finds Alfhild sitting on the floor in a slightly unraveled lotus position. *Affi-Bee?* She opens her eyes, and for a moment he just stands there and drips, letting the seawater pool on the linoleum floor. *It's cold in here, don't you think?* He drapes her red jacket around her shoulders and puts a small pot of water on the stove to boil. *Feeling sad today?* He looks at her quickly as he reaches for the cups. Her face is pale and completely impassive. She watches him stir the cocoa mix into the water, then, after taking a sip, she grimaces slightly and puts the cup down. *You miss Grandma?*

She adjusts the position of her legs, moving her heels closer to her abdomen, inhaling slowly through her nose. She closes her eyes and places her hands on her knees, her palms turned upward, and asks: *Who?*

He watches her breathe, and much later, during a PIPRAD support group meeting in the back of a café above the old pharmacy in Østergade, he describes the movement of her shoulders—the slight rise and fall of her jacket—as a pulse, as a pale-red jellyfish undulating in a vast expanse of blue. He looks down at the Styrofoam cup in his hands. Even though there are other episodes, more dramatic and far more frightening, especially during her university years, this is the moment he recalls most clearly: *It was our first real scare.*

The group facilitator asks if that was the experience that pushed them to change her medication. He shakes his head. *We switched to MetaSerenalinne after a serious incident a few years ago; we still use it every now and again with a mild over-the-counter inhibitor.*

A woman called Lisbeth dabs her nose with a Kleenex and begins to speak: *After three months on MetaSerenalinne, my teenage son gained twenty-five pounds and developed breasts. It destroys the libido too; they use it in the prison system to chemically castrate sex offenders.*

She pauses to sniffle, and the woman next to her asks: *So what if it destroys the libido? You know expressive sarcastics don't have sex, don't you?*

Lisbeth blows her nose and replies through the Kleenex: *Oh, but they do, Ulrikke, they just don't enjoy it.* There are wry smiles and chuckles, and before the group facilitator can stop it, a discussion erupts about whether expressive sarcastics shrug when they climax or just wrinkle their noses and go: *Meh.* The laughter is distressing to some, but to most middle-aged parents of PIPRAD children, it is all there is left; each *ha ha* and *tee-hee* a hole in an airtight box, a warm dot of light in which you can sit and just close your eyes for a moment.

HE GOES THROUGH Alfhild's apartment, emptying ashtrays, opening windows, pruning the clutter on the tables and floor, plucking unopened envelopes and mugs furry with mold from nests of paper and plastic detritus. When he is done with the vacuuming and the wiping down, he wraps a towel around Alfhild's shoulders and washes her hair in the kitchen sink. She closes her eyes as he massages her scalp. Sometimes, when he needs to re-assess the effect of the MetaSerenalinne, he very gently provokes her. Today he pretends to pull things out of her hair. A ribbon of seaweed. A dried-up shark's egg. A flat moss-covered stone.

She tenses and raises her head from the sink. *What's that?*

With the tip of his finger, he flattens the shampoo suds that stick to the moss. *From the Japanese rock garden? Don't you remember?*

As she sits up and leans forward, her long, graying hair flops over her shoulders and water starts trickling onto the chair. Dark spots spread on her sweatpants and slippers. She looks at the stone in his hand. *Okay, Dad, your turn, guess what this is.* She shows him the top of her head, parting her hair with her fingers.

I don't see anything, Alfhild. He fumbles for his glasses. *I can't even see the old scars anymore.*

She makes a sound like a game-show buzzer. *Wrong, Dad, these are not scars, they're ballistic striations.* He asks her what she means, and with a roll of her eyes, she explains: *From being born, Dad, you know, the unique scratch patterns in my scalp from when I shot out of Mom's rifled birth canal.* The game goes on. Other strange analogies are drawn, but none as striking and as viscerally disturbing as the idea of childbirth as the firing of a living, breathing bullet. The image stays with him for weeks. He worries about her mental equilibrium, the inescapable unwholesomeness of self-identifying as a bullet. For several nights, he has dreams about Clara giving birth, about doctors and nurses diving for cover as Alfhild ricochets off the walls, breaking overhead lights and monitor screens— whenever he tries to get in her way, she contorts her trajectory, swerving around him, and so he just stands there, in the flickering dimness of the delivery room, waving his arms and swaying his torso in a futile attempt to intercept her with his chest.

It is not uncommon, he later finds out, for parents of expressive sarcastics to think of their children as dangerous things that fly through the air. In a low, continuous monotone, Lisbeth describes her son as an asteroid, headed straight toward Earth: *A world-ending event, that's how I saw him before the medication and the behavioral therapy. It slowed him down, reduced him, and now, when I close my eyes, instead of a huge fire-rimmed shape in the sky, I see a rock on the ground.* She pauses, pressing her lips together.

You sound disappointed, the group facilitator says.

Well, yes, he's a goddamn rock on the ground.

Ulrikke interjects: *So, you prefer the end of the world, is that what you're saying?*

Ignoring the question, Lisbeth turns to Alfhild's father and smiles. *Could we go back to your dream for a moment?*

Before he can answer, Ulrikke gets up from her seat and declares that untreated irony is as harmful as smoking eighteen cigarettes a day. Lisbeth responds by describing the side effects of what she refers to as chemically induced perceptual castration.

Bo raises his hand. Without relaxing the straight-backed posture he has quietly maintained for almost an hour, he looks up at Ulrikke and says in a deep, sorrowful voice: *Irony is the poisonous plant that you eat every day so you can suffer and die with a smile on your face.* Something in Bo's hazel-gray eyes makes Ulrikke sit down. She smooths her skirt with the palms of her hands. She crosses her legs. Then she blushes ever so slightly.

Lisbeth gives a loud laugh and says that there's nothing like a good folksy aphorism to make a woman go weak in the knees, to which Bo responds: *I teach meditation, Eastern philosophy, and various martial arts.*

He shows no signs of discomfort as Lisbeth nods and leans forward, inspecting the flat, calloused knuckles of his hands and the contours of his biceps and chest. He even turns his head to one side when she holds up a finger and rotates her wrist. *You know, if you're going to fight him, Ulrikke, you should just grab that thing and pull as hard as you can.*

The long, grizzled ponytail swivels back, and Bo, exuding an air of imperturbable calm, inhales through his nose and says very softly: *Enough about me.*

After the meeting, Bo catches up with Alfhild's father outside. *That was a real privilege.* Bo places his hand flat on his chest. *Thank you, thank you for inviting me and for sharing so openly during the session.*

Forcing a smile, Alfhild's father begins to move forward and says: *We've shared so much already, so why not this?*

Bo nods in solemn agreement. *Yes, true, very true.*

For a while, they walk down Østergade without speaking—side by side—Alfhild's father setting the pace. Out of the corner of his eye, he notices Bo turning his head, looking away. There is a sharp intake of air followed by several sobs and a high-pitched whine that fades into sniffles. They stop between a tea shop and a foot-shaped chiropodist's sign. *It's too . . . every . . . everything is . . .* Bo is bawling again, and Alfhild's father—unable to watch a large, muscular man cry in the street—just stands there, hand on his forehead, eyes fixed on the tips of his shoes.

Eventually, as the sobbing continues, he pats Bo on the elbow and says: *I know, champ. I know.*

This is the promise he made to Clara: to attend a support group, and for the first year, at least once every month, to go together with Bo. *And try not to be hateful,* she whispered, reaching up to take hold of his hand, gripping two of his fingers and the lower half of his palm.

Try not to be hateful. Even in extremis, Clara's expectations of him remained resolutely levelheaded and low.

The day after Clara came back from the hospital, Bo called and said that she wanted to see him—wanted him to be part of the process—and so for almost a week, they took turns sitting with her during the night. Alfhild kept to herself, spending most of her time in her old room upstairs, sleeping and writing. One night, they saw her stand in the corridor, peeking into the bedroom, the frame of the doorway revealing only her shoulder and part of her face. As Clara tried to speak, Alfhild stepped forward and made finger-gun gestures, firing several shots at them both. Then she went back to her room. *She'll be all right.* He squeezed Clara's hand. *She's stronger now, she'll be okay.*

Clara made a soft broken sound, and in her face, he saw shameful relief, he saw tight, tiny muscles guiltily loosening up at the edge of her eyes and her mouth as she sighed: *I'm sorry to do this to you.*

All parents with a single PIPRAD child must confront this fact: only one of you will be able to die secure in the knowledge that your clinically unlovable child will not be alone in the world. Though he has never said it out loud or even articulated the thought in his head, Alfhild's father has always taken for granted that he would be first. With his hypertension, multiple cancer scares, and dots on his brain scans, how could he not? He is not envious of Clara, but there is disappointment, he cannot deny it, a grim sense of missed opportunity. Still, the grief-stricken mind is a smooth, inexorable thing, and soon it slips forward in time—three or four years, probably less—to show him his own freshly dug grave, and there he sees Alfhild, unwashed and forlorn, looking down at his headstone while she claps very slowly: *Great job, Dad, way to go.*

It pains him, of course, to imagine a future like that, and so after another PIPRAD support group meeting, he tries to be pleasant, nodding and smiling benignly whenever Bo shares his opinions on self-contemplation and dealing with grief. By the end of the year, he is grateful to Clara for her dying wish. He sees Bo's usefulness; his influence on Alfhild, his role in her world as a comforting presence—large and uncomplaining—like a bridge or a pale, featureless hill. It is snowing as they step outside, but Bo does not seem to notice: *Don't worry, she's not a disturbance, she just sits in the corner watching the afternoon classes, just, you know, Affi being Affi, meditating and scribbling away in her notebook. I can't really say I understand her writing, but her imagination is truly ferocious, I'm sure you agree.* A woman from the support group makes eye contact as she walks by, and Bo beams back at her, waving his hand.

Well, I wouldn't know, Alfhild's father says. *She never shows me her writing.*

Bo gives him a look. *Never?*

More attendees come out the door. On the stone steps outside the building, Lisbeth breaks free from a small group of women and crosses the parking lot. She smiles at Alfhild's father, pulling her coat tighter around her. Then she rubs her gloved hands and looks up at Bo: *It's freezing out here, come on, let's go, let's go.*

It's unclear when it started exactly, but in Alfhild's opinion it started too soon: *You don't know him like I do, Dad, I bet they were already doing it while Mom was dying.* She stares at him from behind the small kitchen table.

That's not possible, Alfhild.

She shakes her head: *I've been to the dojo, I've seen his so-called self-defense classes for women.* With a dismissive scoop of the hand, she describes a room full of big-bosomed housewives lying on their backs, practicing eye-gouging and fish-hooking and knees to the groin. *He's going from student to student like some ponytailed rooster, and the looks they're giving him, Dad, it's fucking grotesque.*

In her voice, there is a wry invitation to play, and he is tempted, of course, to indulge her, but instead of just egging her on with an insincere statement about Bo not being that bad, he hears himself say: *How will you remember me, Alfhild, years from now?*

She holds his gaze for a moment, surprised and annoyed by the abrupt change of subject. She wrinkles her nose and looks away. When he asks her again, a slight tremor in his voice makes her upper lip curl. She points at his face. *Okay, stop, Dad, that look you're giving me now, it's like . . . ugh, like a handwritten note on a door in a restroom.* Still pointing, she draws a square in the air with her finger and reads aloud: *Out of order, please don't look.* He sputters with laughter at this roundabout way of calling him broken and full of crap, but later, over the following months, the idea of the note begins to perturb him. He sees it whenever he looks at himself in the mirror. He carries it with him, and in the spring when he finds himself in the hallway of Lisbeth's old timber-framed house, he is aware of being cautiously scrutinized, the note still stuck to his forehead, its small shameful squiggles glued to his skin.

Relax, this is a party. Lisbeth grins and helps him out of his coat. *The whole family, together at last.*

Bo asks him what he wants to drink, and Lisbeth introduces him to her son, Sofus, a short man with jowls and a pronounced double chin, his expression a blend of bulldog and Buddha. The son shakes his hand without a word.

Sofus is thinking about going back to law school next year, Lisbeth explains with a joyous little laugh.

And in the meantime, Bo is teaching him nunchucks, Alfhild chimes in, glancing at Sofus, who refuses to acknowledge her presence. Alfhild turns in her chair. *Look, Dad.* She gestures at the gold and silver balloons taped to the wall in the shape of a heart. *Look what they made me.*

Alfhild's father places a small white envelope on the table in front of her. *Happy birthday, Alfhild.*

She scrunches her nose. *Thanks, Dad. I'll open it later, okay?*

He nods. He reaches for his glass, and whenever he drinks, he feels his old steel watch drop from his wrist to the crook of his elbow. When Alfhild goes outside to smoke, he gets the first tentative question about the procedure. He lies about the probable outcome but leaves most of the facts starkly unaltered. A solemn expression forms on Bo's face. They talk about Alfhild. Both Bo and Lisbeth make one extravagant promise after the other, and later at the hospital, when Alfhild's father thinks back on this moment, he remembers Sofus looking up from the game on his phone, his earbuds still leaking faraway gunshots and the faint sounds of a car chase. Then comes his voice, deep and serene: *I will watch over her, too, old man, for your sake I will love her.* It is not real, Alfhild's father knows this, of course, it is a dream, a chimera of infinite compassion, a nurse had warned him that this might happen, that some of the painkillers might ever so slightly scramble his brain— those were her words, *ever so slightly.*

He hears the nurse in the hallway, communicating with someone in a secretive whisper. Alfhild enters his room alone. As she stands by the bedside, smelling of smoke, she points at his face and utters her usual deathbed salute: a loud, mocking, singsong-syllable-stretching *haw–haw.* This has become a routine, a strange little ritual so inherently grim that it feels kind of sacred. With an abusive remark, she pulls up a chair and begins to dissect his countless shortcomings. For as long as he can, he tries to hold on to the sound of her voice. Then his eyes close, and he feels the heat of the sun directly above him. On the path to the beach, he casts no shadow at all. The day is hot, the sand burns his feet as he climbs the last dune, and there, at the water's edge, he sees her, five years old, the tight rubber band of her prescription swim goggles squashing her hair at the back of her head. A wave washes over her feet. Her shoulders tense. She turns and sends him a look that says: *Dad, what should I do?* He holds out his hand. *Go on in, Affi-Bee, I'll be here.* She looks back at the sea and trembles, rubbing her arms as though she were cold or trying to calm herself down. Another wave reaches her. The water ripples around her ankles. Her toes disappear in the sand. She raises her arm and points at something on the horizon. A dark speck in the water. He is not sure what it is. Alfhild keeps pointing as it moves farther and farther away.

Alex Boeden lives in a quiet corner of Scandinavia.

Editor's Note

The first thing that drew our editors' interest to this story was Felix's bold choice to have the narrator tell her story in Trinidadian vernacular. The language is both open enough for any English reader to follow it and closed enough to convey the narrator's deepest emotions, not to mention a whole culture. Indeed, this story is an education in "the cutass process," where, depending on the offense, you might "get blows like Bobolee Friday"; how to "river lime" in the wilder places of Trinidad; what it means "to catch she self"; what a soucouyant is; and what obzuckie means—as in the donated clothes the narrator had to wear were so big and obzuckie that the kids at her new high school made fun of them.

"Return to Sender: Big Time Tief" deals with the subject of families that are ruptured by the forces of late-stage capitalism and must contend with the difficult repair after those ruptures. The narrator, Chrissy, is a recent immigrant, torn between two countries and cultures. Does she want to live with her mother in the United States or in Trinidad with her aunt who has raised her for ten years? Where is the love? She had never wanted to come live with her mother, but now that she has arrived, the longing for her mother—who has continued to be absent despite her proximity—is painful and poignant. Though the lyrical language captivated us from the start, it was this complex relationship between mother and daughter that made this story moving and memorable. There are no easy answers in this story, but after having read it, and one asks oneself again *Where is the love?*, the answer is patent—in Chrissy, the narrator, definitely.

Tanya Larkin, Managing Editor
Transition Magazine

Return to Sender: Big Time Tief

Winelle Felix

I SEE THIS THING DANGLING. SO SHINY, IT DIDN'T
have any strings attached. Yes, it was in the people and dem store,
but I ain't see no security tab attach to it. To me, it look like they
was giving it away. I just slipped the bracelet into my jeans' back
pocket and walked out. No alarm went off, nothing. Easy like
Sunday morning. Like it was dey waiting for me all them years.
Just like how people feel they family up in America waiting for
them with no strings attached.

Ah make it out the store and now ah was feeling bad. I wanted
to carry it back, but I wasn't that stupid. To actually get catch was
like playing with bushfire—the spread of them flames is uncon-
trollable. Once it start, ain't no stopping. And if I get catch, the
bushfire was meh mother. Next thing yuh know, I carry the thing
back and instead of them letting me go, they call meh mother. That
just sounds like pure madness.

If Miss Beatrice Elvira Roberts, AKA Patsy, had to come downtown Boston to get me from Macy's because she get a call from the
security guard saying they catch me stealing, all hell would break
loose. Ah start to walk faster in the direction of the bus stop one
time. Crossing the road, I clutch my jean jacket tighter, bracing my
chest for the cold. The fall breeze seeping through meh jacket like
a strainer. Ah put one hand in meh back pocket to feel the ridges,

scrunch so tightly together. Making it resemble the touch of them big piece of nutcake we use to get when Auntie church use to have Thanksgiving.

I could see Mummy, clear as day, in the people and dem store. Begging the security guard and the store manager to let me go. The security, probably from the Caribbean, too, would understand my deserving fate. Probably bad-talking meh in he head: *Look at she, giving all ah we ah bad name. That is what alyuh does come in the people and dem country to do—Tief? Hmmm. Such ah damn shame.*

And while he and the store manager deliberating, the security guard, with he so-called self-righteousness, of course his intentions would be to make sure I don't shame the rest of the Caribbean people living in Boston or prevent them who trying to get they visas— from getting it. He can't allow one bad apple to spoil it for rest. Ah sure he go be shouting: *Lock she ass up and throw away the key.*

That is, until he see Mummy ninja skills through the corner of he eye. Effortlessly drawing for she sword, gliding she shoes off, lancing one blow to the back of meh head, without concern for him or anybody else in the room. Is then, and only then, he would feel at ease to coax the store manager, with she wiggly golden curls bouncing like Alice in Wonderland: *We need to get rid of these people before a bigger crime occurs.* And with pitying eyes, the store manager would agree and let us go.

Zooming around the corner to catch the bus, I almost run into this white guy pose up by the wall. He ain't have time to study me. He quickly go back to quarreling with his thoughts, every now and then puffing he cigarette for relief from whatever jumbie he have on him. I see a few people waiting to get the bus too. Just now there will be more, come rush hour.

Not by a long shot, the bacchanal would stop they in Macy's. After we leave the store, I imagine, Mummy giving the Dimanche Gras performance of she life. She go be dead smack in the middle of the people and dem road between Macy's and the army store downtown Boston, carrying on like a madwoman. Thank God the traffic cuts off by the corner so pedestrians could walk downtown in a kinda laissez-faire manner without worrying about getting bounced down. To tell yuh the truth, I don't think she would even move if it wasn't so.

And is so the parade would start. Mummy trailing behind me, cussing stinker than ah drunken sailor come carnival Monday. The empty clash of plastic—itching meh ear every time her hands fight the air. Drenched in costume jewelry—dripping and dangling like some drug man's girlfriend from Laventille. Her makeup would be done, of course. She wouldn't just leave the house anyhow. What if she bounced-up Janice and dem? *Yuh mad, I can't have people looking at me anyhow—we're not in Trinidad anymore, sweetie.*

One of she favorite lines she love to sing, in attempt to help me understand how things work up here in America. Along with: *Is this what ah bring you up to America for?* Or *If is embarrassment yuh want, is embarrassment ah go give yuh.*

Pacing back and forth behind the crowd that started to gather by the bus stop, just wishing by chance the bus would come early. What if someone saw me when ah pick up the bracelet? What if they saw meh face on the cameras and they are printing out my picture right now, and they coming to look for me. Let put my hoodie up. Thinking about how easy it was of course it must ah been ah trap all along.

And now the damn bus couldn't come fast enough. It would be

good to have some extra time with Mummy too. I know she getting ready for work about this time. Ah have a few minutes to catch she, just now she go be rushing out the door for her night shift at Mass General Hospital. She is ah cleaner for them. If I ain't see she in that window, well boy, I ain't seeing she till tomorrow around this time. School does start so damn early, plus travel time. Is ah bus, ah train, then another bus, so by the time I leave her in the morning, Mummy half-dead asleep. Mouth open just wide enough to fit a pencil.

Of course, Mummy wouldn't understand why I had to tief the bracelet. All she would be looking for is an answer. The most appropriate plaster for the sore: *Is this what ah bring you up to America for?*

Yuh see—Mummy wouldn't really want me to answer this question. Any real Caribbean child know, answer-back is the fastest way to start the cutass process. There's no real guarantee that if yuh don't answer the question that yuh ass might get spare. In my opinion, they still going and beat yuh ass anyway. Is just something they like to say to hear theyself talk.

Sometimes, is about how serious the crime is too. And at that point, depending on how bad it is, it ain't matter what yuh say, or if Jesus come down, yuh cutass book. And at that point, is more about the right pot spoon, hanger, telephone cord, or slipper available to deliver the punishment. And *PARTNER*—just brace yuh ass for the blows, doh even bother fight-up and make things worse. And if Mummy was to find out the shit I was doing in the people and dem store, this was definitely going to be me—getting blows like Bobolee Friday.

For a second I imagine losing meh mind and answering she

back, playing brave in the people and dem America, because no-body ain't know me up here. My hands in the air, too, like we both playing mas downtown Boston: *What's the big deal? Nobody saw me put the bracelet in my pocket, so who am I hurting? Who's going to miss it? What you don't know can't hurt you, and out of sight, out of mind. You would know, right!*

THE DAY AUNTIE tell me ah get through with meh visa, I thought it was ah joke she was making. That time, Patricia, D, and Pantin, and I started hanging heavy. Pantin just ask meh to be his gyal, after months of busting style on him, I finally give him a chance. CXC exams was right around the corner, so dem teachers ain't have time to study we.

Every Friday we ducking school to go river-lime up Caura. Oh gosh boy, those was the days.

I told Auntie I ain't want to come up America in a big, big frenzy. I see she packing the maroon grip with pepper sauce and tamarind balls she make for Mummy, unlike she, meh tears was stinging my eyes in protest; is then I realize this thing serious. I real beg she to tell Mummy I want to stay. She raise she voice not too high because I never hear she yell. But for some reason, she felt like she had to that time. She pull my arms and cautioned me to sit on the bed.

When she eyes started to glare-up like when you watch the sun for too long, or like when you unexpectedly bite the piece of bird-pepper yuh forget yuh put in the chow. That wetness gathered dey like pothole puddles after rain—collecting mosquitoes. Right in the corner of she eye. Stagnant. In an unusually softer tone now, softer than pink cotton candy melting in yuh mouth, holding my slick face, she started to plead:

Yuh mother misses you. Ah done already keep you longer than we had talk about. It was just until she catch she self. When yuh mother first left because yuh father say yuh is not he child. And the ten-day-work wasn't coming fast enough. Ah tell she to go to America and ah go mine yuh for a few years until she could send for yuh. Them few years turn into ten years. How that go look if I tell the lady ah keeping she child? Eh, Crissy? Yuh ain't miss yuh mother? Yuh only hearing she voice by phone? How yuh think yuh mother go feel? I don't want to hear nothing else. Yuh going to meet yuh mother. And that's that!

LATER THAT SAME day she call to check to see how the shipping of she child was going. I was in the kitchen trying to stuff down a cheese-paste sandwich Auntie made for me when I hear Mummy tell Auntie to put me the phone: *Crissy, come here, yuh mother want to talk to yuh!*

Yes, Mummy. She start to plead she case now:

What is this business about you not wanting to come up here with me? Oh! Yuh want to stay in Trinidad? For what? You must be out of yuh mind! So you don't think I miss you? You don't think after all these years, I don't want meh child? I want to spend time with you. I want to make up for lost time. Watch that show you be watching all the time. "Law and something." I miss meh child. I sacrifice a lot for them papers to get fix up for yuh to come up the road.

So for me to come up to America and embarrass she by answering she back in front of these people, I'm sure she would jump out she skin like ah soucouyant.

What you say? Turning she whole head around to make sure I was talking to she.

If yuh was in Trinidad, yuh think yuh could ah talk to me so? Yuh so lucky yuh not in Trinidad or else I would ah beat yuh ass already.

As if this was going to save me. I'm sure in the same breath, probably turn around and pitch the Coach moccasins at meh head like she was playing cricket. By this time, people would be looking because there would be no more walking to do. We would have reach the bus stop. And of course, all these people watching will mean nothing to her. She, ranting and raving like she singing the chorus from ah Road March Soca tune, and we crossing the stage making our best attempt to wow the judges. She tune, louder now:

Ah shoulda forget about yuh ass down dey—den yuh woulda know what America is really like! Yuh ain't know what I do to bring yuh ass up here. And this is what you come up to America to do to me? Alyuh think America is so so so easy. I want this, I want that, alyuh have no idea what people have to do to get these things, but yuh come here to tief—and is so the chorus would ring on repeat, probably on till ah turn ah big woman. She would never, ever forget this. I could be a big woman with children and she probably would still say, *Yuh member the time I had to drag yuh ass out of Macy's for stealing?*

This speech. The climax. Like a bust WASA main pipe, leaking in the middle of the road. The blows would rain down on me right dey by the Silver Line bus stop. Going and coming, like there's no tomorrow. Until the water pressure calms down on its own because nobody ain't coming to fix that pipe anytime soon. Yuh go wake up in the morning and see the water still running down the road and wonder if yuh could save this water for the dry season, when water ain't coming at tall.

I wouldn't be too embarrassed, though, because it is not like I am back home, where everybody knows everybody. And if yuh get yuh ass wash in the middle of downtown Port of Spain, expect the whole school to know by tomorrow before you even walk in the homeroom.

America is too big. Nobody have time to run people's business. I don't even know my neighbor next door. As far as I know, there's a ghost next door that cooks fish a lot and watches sports a lot. I know the TV channels more than anything else.

I came up. Mummy enrolled me in some school Janice tell she about. She gave meh the lecture: *Doh embarrass meh. And doh do anything stupid for meh to have to leave work to come and get yuh ass.* She travel with meh on the bus, once. She said she was only able to get one day off from work while showing meh the numbers on the bus to take.

That same friend drop off a bag of old people's clothes the same week for me to wear. Clothes smelling like mildew and camphor balls. I had to wash dem clothes until Mummy quarrel with me to stop, talking about I don't pay no bills here.

If yuh see dem clothes. Some big and obzuckie, what couldn't fit had to turn into home clothes. Because where the new clothes coming from? Not from she. Over and over, Mummy done already made it clear: *I ain't bring you up here to show off for people back home. If you think you come here to be wearing the latest brands, yuh lie. Alyuh feel money does grow on trees in America. Any new clothes you want, you have to buy it with your money. So when you start making money, when you get a job, when you turn sixteen, after you help me with some bills, whatever is left over is what you could buy clothes with. Until then, those clothes will have to do. Because alyuh feel free things hanging on trees up here in America.*

You see, Mummy have no idea how dem children does look at me funny in school. Day in, day out—come these Yankees asking questions. All up in meh face like if I is ah lab rat: *What are you wearing?* I can't even respond without dem saying: *What did you say?* Or *Why do you sound like that?*

Hear Auntie when I give she ah call on WhatsApp to complain: *Not to worry yuh self, darling. Just give it some time, man! Rome wasn't built in ah day, darling. Doh worry, babes, everything go be fine. Just now yuh tongue go be switching better than dem Yankee and dem, soon and very soon you'll be ah Yankee too.*

My accent thicker than molasses and condensed milk. I doubt that happening anytime soon. What I really wanted to say to dem is *Haul yuh mother ass!* But they wouldn't get that either. So I does just swallow meh pride and walk away. Or I does just sit at the back of the class in the corner with my hoodie up and my head down on the table so nobody will bother me. Mummy just ain't know half the shit that does be going on in school.

Come weekend-end, after we clean the lunch-box apartment to the heights of Barron and Kitchener, talking about women wining up and man horning, you know, we kinda thing. All she care about after is feteing with Janice and dem later that night.

When she get up from she siesta in the afternoon, when you hear "Tonight the Blackman Feeling to Party" jamming from the CD player in the bedroom, you know is time for the show to start. This is usually the time I take off the TV from watching reruns of *Law & Order* and creep my way down to her bedroom. Who would want to miss this show?

I usually watch her for a little bit, peeping through the door slit. This is the time of day when the sun filters through the blinds and you see the dust floating in the air. And you wonder if dey were there all the time. She, wining down to the ground as she flings outfits onto the bed to try. After a couple spins, she usually noticed me spying: *Don't just stand dey maccoing my business. Come let me show yuh how it's done. Don't feel because I'm up here all these years I can't still shake it* . . . She then puts she hands on she head, lifts up her leg like she in a mas band, and starts to throw waist like a spinning top.

Is the end for me I does revel in. Is ah kinda magic. You have to be there to see. Maybe it's the way she puts on her red-lipstick heels and test she balance as she wine down to the ground one last time. Or maybe it's the way the Marlboros in she mouth does be slouching to the side, eyes in ah hazy sleep but still seeing everything. I can't decide which one na. All I know is when she shoos me to the cabinet to go make the nastiest mac and cheese I have ever tasted in meh life for dinner, I know the show is over.

If she's in a good mood, a little further along, I'll get a little better ending. If her words drag on the floor and the sweaty glass of liquor next to the blunt empty, I know things are shaping up for a better ending. She will say: *Ah leaving a few dollars on top of the dresser. Dey for yuh to order a pizza later eh!* And plant a nice red-lipstick sticker on meh cheeks. *Don't wash that off eh.* Then springs off the bed to take one last look in the mirror before she heads out. She looking and tracing she shape, trying to smooth out her clothes. While she picks up the phone to call Janice: *Alyuh ready, girl, ah coming out for alyuh tonight. Alyuh ain't ready for me tonight nah* . . . Then busting out the most coskel laugh you will ever hear.

Although she claims she has no money when I ask her for new clothes, money never missing when she see the Sprangerman park up by Tropical Grocery store, though. *What you have for me today, darling?* And we must go by Tropical every Sunday. Is the only store in Boston where you can get yuh pigtails and callaloo bush and mostly anything Caribbean. She would never tell Janice where she really gets she Gucci belts from. What for? Lies are better than truths.

And the truth is, *Life in America is better than life in Trinidad— welcome to the American Dream* is what people use to say, including Auntie when they talk about America. Now that ah up here, that is neither here nor there with me. The jury is still out on that one for me. What I do know, is this: *wearing the latest Gucci knockoff and having your friends and dem believe it is real is better than any life you could think of.* That is what Mummy say: *in this America, you have to fake it until you could make it.*

She eyes always full of bags under dem. Maybe is the bags from work, or always having to look good for people up here and in Trinidad just so she could post pictures on Facebook. I ain't know na.

But if you does hear she when she talking about people in Trinidad, loud loud in she room: *Gyal! I still look better compared to dem burn-up people in Trinidad. My complexion even now. I ain't have to run up and down in the hot sun. Running to catch maxi or running after man.* But now she was running after something else, because she never home. Not even on the weekends.

BEFORE AMERICA, I ain't have time to study these things. I find myself always thinking-thinking now. Trinidad is a simple life. Is school, bust ah lime, church with Auntie, and that's about it. But that's not how things work up here. You have to think and think until you figure out life in America.

Sometimes you find yuhself thinking so much you don't even remember how you get home. Yuh never know yuh could think so much. You think so much about yuh friends and the life you once knew, that yuh find yuhself physically shaking your head trying to shake them thoughts out. Yuh know it doh make sense, but yuh still try. Fuss yuh head heavy with thoughts. But all this shaking does is just make yuh think about dem more. You wonder mostly if Pantin and them will ever remember you.

I check the time on the bus stop monitor, it say: *Bus arrives in 5 minutes.* A few more people gather at the bus stop. I imagine they are thinking-thinking too. Because no one talks to anyone in America. Unless you crazy, and then you still talking to yuhself because no one answering yuh. We just listening to yuh business.

Is not like in Trinidad when yuh home alone, yuh could go and find a neighbor. Yuh could take a walk by the corner and bust ah lime. Can't do that in America. The first time ah went shoplifting, right in a Walgreens a couple blocks from meh house, nobody was home as usual. Loneliness eating meh whole. I went for a walk in search of some kind of company. Ah say let me take a walk down by the Walgreens to get some Häagen-Dazs Rum Raisin ice cream to finish the *Law & Order* marathon I was watching.

One Boyo-looking dark-skin security guard keep he eyes steady and focus on me. I acted normal—not too fast, not too slow. I had to act as if I was shopping my life away. I wanted to spite him too. Like why he only looking at me. So much people in the store and is only me yuh want to macco. I could feel his stare lingering like the leftover heat on a hot day back home. He must not know where I come from—heat is nothing. Where I'm from the heat taunts you all day, then waits for you at night in your pillows and sheets—you dear not expect it t' leave. So who he thought he was, I welcomed it. Long time I ain't feel that kind of heat since coming to the States.

I WAIT TILL he stop watching. Take the ice cream and put it in my big-ass puffy jacket from Janice bags. It was the most useful piece of clothing in them set of old clothes. I walk out the store and then sprint all the way home. I didn't catch meh breath till ah reach home, ah reach the steel door to meh apartment. Talk about excitement rushing through meh head. That ice cream never tasted so good.

I started off slow, though. I realized if yuh buy some stuff sometimes to distract dem, they usually don't bother yuh. Always keep the receipt visible so they could see when yuh walking out the store. I wasn't into big items like clothes—too much steps. Yuh have to remove the security tab so it doesn't make noise, go to the dressing room to switch it out. Is just too much fuss.

I feel like I was ready for something bigger today. When this white girl came up to me today at lunch and watch me dry in my face so, turn and tell me to go back to meh country, I said you know what, she was right. I didn't even think to knock she ass out. I thought she had a point.

After school, I stopped in by Macy's a bit, just looking at handbags, shoes, pillowcases. Everything yuh could think about. All ah bunch of unnecessary stuff to keep yuh company when the night come. Is just so Mummy room does be looking. Sometimes I find meh self talking to the bags and them and pretending that they is

Pantin and them when ah home alone watching TV in Mummy's room.

When I slip the jewelry off the hook, about a good half an hour ago, I was thinking that today of all days I deserve a little gift for meh self. It resembled the one Mummy had on she foot. I could put it on to go to school and she wouldn't even notice. I just had to get it. I walked out with it like it was nothing.

THIS MORNING I got up early and I couldn't fall back to sleep. I hear mamie creep in a little earlier than usual. The wooden floors crying under she weight. Whispering on the phone to Janice about the upcoming weekend. Janice's loud mouth belching through the speaker: *What you wearing this weekend, girl?*

I ain't know nah! She walks in her room and close the door. I hear voices, sharper now through the cardboard walls, drowning out the life outside meh window starting to wake. The streetlight fading away as the morning peak, pearls of cloudy cotton balls start to form in the sky. Make no sense sleeping. I have school in a few hours. I hear the hangers scratching the closet bar as she ramsack she clothes to take a look: *I have a see-through turtleneck top. I'll wear with these new jeans I buy from Macy's the other day.*

I hear the noise tiptoeing *(Yeah, girl, that go look real good to-gether . . . Yuh go mash them up with that outfit).*

Hey, are you up?

Yeah.

Did you take my new jeans to try on and forget to put it back? I told you about looking through my stuff? Did you? Did you take it?

No, Patsy, I don't have yuh jeans?

Oh yeah, by the way . . . I have something to tell you.

Yessss!

Ah spending Saturday night out eh! Yuh ain't seeing meh till Sunday evening. I'll leave some change for yuh to order Domino's.

So we not going to Tropical Sunday morning?

Na!

I just slide down under the cover and turn around to the glare coming from the window. Wishing I could hear the wild fowl from we neighbor Jerome bought as pet from Arima Market. I remember when he first get the thing. We use to cuss him about it. Saying we go steal it and make stew chicken. Until we all get use to it. We all started throwing food for it whenever we pass by. I wonder if it still living. Same time, I hear a bling echo through the room: message from Auntie. I click off the screen and ignore.

Before I leave for school, I creep into Mummy room. I see the outfit she was talking about. Her blue work shirt dash on the floor, and one of her legs hanging off the bed.

I LIFT SHE foot to put it back on the bed. I see the chain barely dancing. It just dey, stiff-stiff. Stifling she ankle—both of them looking like chunky pig feet. The chain twist up, decorating the swelling in a cute way. She's so dead to the world. She spirit traveling. She doesn't even move when I untwist the anklet. I try to make it look pretty again against her bruised veins, the color of rum prunes for black cake.

This bus really need to hurry so I could see her. I was starting to get worried the bus was running off scheduled. Where the hell is this bus? It would have been here already. Today of all days. They usually send out a bus before, to curb the rush-hour madness. People are just standing there looking off into their thoughts too.

I walk over to the bench. I like sitting close to the edge, as to be ready to move when the crowds pack in or some kinda bacchanal break out. Looking around now, I think I see the security guard from Macy's to the corner of my eye ducking around the corner.

When I had first come into the store, I notice him standing in front of the doors. His glasses chunky like magnifying glasses. His sharp white shirt tucked neatly in his river-cut trousers. I get up right away. I don't chance it. Shit, he probably have the paper with meh face on it and he coming to look for meh. I escape through an alleyway between the buildings and end up on the other side, where there's a CVS in front, right as you walk out. I enter and walk around a bit. I start from the back. I make my way up and down the aisles, hiding behind customers. Constantly looking around me to see if there's any white shirts coming. This one old lady ask meh if I'm all right. I guess I didn't realize I wasn't looking all right. Maybe this is the day it all catches up to me.

With barely a green card, today would be the day I would make my way back to Trinidad. If I got caught, deportation was sure and I would never be able to see Mummy again. Mummy was for sure sending meh ass home. Not like ah does see she now anyways. She wasn't even fix properly either. She always telling meh when yuh answer the house phone and someone ask for Patsy, tell dem she not home—either way, I was going home because she wouldn't want to be mixed up in this because as she self always singing: *I put in too many years in this country, I going and get my sacrifice back, by the hook or the crook!*

I still had time to pick back up right way we left off with Pantin
and dem. We use to meet up behind the school and cut through the
hole in the fence by the sour-cherry tree. Sun so hot it would make
our breath melt. Sun too hot for school, so we would skip that. We
would lime by the banga tree down by the river. Ripples made by
wind would rock the dark-green water back and forth, absorbing
the heat, the tree leaves would dance and the birds would sing their
lullabies.

If I get caught, she would have to send me back home for Auntie to finish take care of me. There's no way she could keep me. She
wouldn't send meh back without a little something, though. For
sure, Mummy would pack my ass in a barrel, faster than I could say
Sorry, Mummy. I don't want to go back home. I want to stay with you.
I could imagine myself stuffed in a barrel, with a letter addressed
to meh Auntie title:

Return to sender:

*Big Time Tief inside, and the things yuh ask for. I go call yuh later
and explain what this wotless girl come up America to do.*

Me at the bottom, of course. Because everybody knows when
you packing a barrel to send back with goods, you have to roll up
the biggest item with the smaller items inside. So that Customs
and dem by the port don't bust yuh head with price. On top of me,
the nasty mac and cheese in the blue box, I can't stand that baby
powder shit. How you could just add water and cheese would ap-
pear? Nasty nasty, never taste anything nasty so. A bunch of those
boxes would be scattered on top of me. On top of that would be
some used knockoff Gucci clothes and belts. Foil and cling wrap,
hair dye and sweet-smelling body splashes from Victoria's Secret,

because all of these things are too expensive to buy in Trinidad but are still necessary somehow.

Ah swing down the hair-grooming aisles and see the spray that Auntie does use to cover up she grays watching meh on the shelf. The lady on the bottle looking nothing like Auntie, not even close. Auntie's face full and round like the lady on Miss Mabel's Green Seasoning bottle. The lady on the spray can hair long like them Indian girls in dey sari for Diwali. I wonder if the company knows that. I look around to see who's close by, swing my handbag to the front of me, and knock the tiny spray can bottle into my bag.

Auntie swears that every store in America is call Walmart. *Just pick up the bottle for meh by Walmart nah.* Up to now, I never even step foot in a Walmart. *Give it some time, man,* she soothes on the phone when I tell her I want to come back home. I want to believe she. But how much time so will it take?

I MISS COMING home to Auntie always being home. Boy, did she have all the time in the world. If she wasn't making uniforms for the children in the neighborhood, she was in church service, and she would drag me right behind she. And if she left before I got home from school to go pray circle, or market for live chickens, or cheese and hops bread or provision for soup, she always make sure and have ah cheese-paste sandwich cover down in the microwave for me. With a note: *Love u Crissy. Made your favorite. Coming back home just now.*

She never married, and she never had children. She would always say when I ask her if she regret not having children, she would always smile, *Well, if I had children yuh little backside wouldn't be so spoil*, and then walk over and pinch my cheeks. I just had to get this bottle for she.

I look at the clock in the front doorway entrance of the store; time was running out. I didn't want to miss the four o'clock bus because then I wouldn't make it home on time to catch Mummy. So instead of lingering any longer, I just chance it and walk right out. Meh heart in meh throat like a frog.

I hear something go off, but I don't stop to check. I hear the *Miss, Miss* in the back of me, first like little stones, then louder like big bricks hitting meh ear. I pause a bit. I know to myself this could be meh one-way ticket. I hear the sound coming closer, the time is now three mins to four. And I just take off running.

I swing the corner and I see the gray tube blocking the front of the alley. I pick up my sprint now. I hear meh phone blinking. I'm out of breath because you know how long I ain't go for a sweat. I ain't have nobody to play football with. But I have to catch this bus to see Mummy or else I wouldn't get meh a good-night kiss until tomorrow. She always kiss me three times, sometimes four. Today might be five. I'm sure she remember by now. She say they are for morning, lunch, and dinner, and the fourth one is for all the years she miss. *Eventually, ah go catch up*, she likes to say as she close the door behind her when she leaves.

Right before the bus pulls off, I start to bang it like we use to bang on the walls in class when we making big-chunes bout dem sketel girls and dem. Or when the teacher ain't come in that day and we just feel like disturbing the class next door. The driver stops. I dash on the bus trying to catch meh breath walking to the

back with meh phone in meh hand. I open up the screen and realize there's another message from Auntie. I open the app and the
first message pops up like, remember me:

*Happy Birthday Crissy, I missing yuh bad girl. All now so yuh
know ah up baking yuh favorite sponge cake. Just wanted to get yuh
before school. I go call yuh later. Love you.*

Then the second: *Ah just calling to wish yuh a Happy Birthday my
love. I hope you are having a wonderful day. I wanted to call since this
morning, but I just send ah text this morning after prayers circle with
pastor and dem. I didn't want to wake you. You behaving yuh self? I
so glad you leave here. Every minute, somebody getting gun down. The
crime rate so high in Trinidad right now. If it's not that then is somebody
girl child walking around with ah big belly. Thank God yuh live to see
another year, so many children down here ain't even have that chance.
Don't forget to work hard in school and stay out of trouble, okay. I can't
wait to see you when you come back. I'm so proud of you do-do darling.
Tell yah mother ah say hi. Love you . . .*

I OPEN MEH bag to make sure the spray was still there. It was. I
start to feel up meh back pocket to make sure the bracelet was
there, too, but I didn't feel anything. Ah start to pat and pat like
I was a madwoman putting out fire on meh backside. I wanted to
retrace my steps, but Mummy must be waiting for me with one
foot out the door. I get up to look on the seat. It is possible it
may have slipped out onto the seat when I sat. There's a man flop-
ping behind the bus. Waving and yelling for the bus driver to stop.
He manages to catch up at the traffic light. He gets on, huffing

and puffing. As if his life depended on this mission. "You could have waited for the other bus, there's another bus right behind!" the driver suggested. The man's urgency was overly dramatic to the bus driver and passengers too. The man didn't respond. He spirited straight to the back of this bus like a messiah, here to deliver a message. His belly bulldozing in front, arms filing behind like Popeye. Charging in my direction, he begins to point at me frantically, yelling, *Miss, Miss, Miss* . . . Leaning over me, dangling this thing. Looking like ah plumb-cheek Statue of Liberty, holding a carrot for me, the horse. *You drop something? It fell out your pocket.* Shining brighter than it was in the store now. The afternoon sun hitting the bus. The man transforming into a tree dangling a juicy Julie mango, ripe and sweet, just waiting to be plucked. As if! As if! Just so, just so. This perfect Julie mango hanging for me. Just so, with no strings attached. He nudge me, in a slower pitch now, ask, *Miss, is this your bracelet?*

I look at his smug face, eyes bright, waiting for an answer. He was so happy he went out of his way to do this one good deed. Causing all this commotion, everybody looking at me. As if I needed this. As if I asked to come up here in America for this. And as if this was the thing I couldn't live without. I got vexed with him for putting my business out there for everybody in the bus to macco.

I wanted to look at him dead smack in he face, get up, too, so he could see me good and proper, and tell him about he self: *You think I want to be up here on this blasted bus picking this force ripe mango from you, all yellow and smooth on the outside and all black and hard in the inside? Eh? With no taste? You think I want that?* I wanted to take the bracelet and pelt it back in he face.

Instead, I put meh head down, looking at my pale, flaky nails. And in a hushing tone tell him *No*. Never look back in his direction. This delay—of course, by now Mummy would have two foot out the door, hustling to go and do the people and them work.

Winelle Felix is a Trinidadian writer living in Boston. She is an MFA candidate in the creative writing program at Emerson College. When she is not translating her experiences through writing, she's thinking of a master plan to get back to Maracas Beach, where she can get her hands on some Bake and Shark.

Editor's Note

As an international magazine, we don't receive many stories that depict the Great Migration and its legacy. Neither do we receive many stories that depict such chilling encounters with white terror; in this one, you'll find as comprehensive a spectrum as occurs in reality, from that which is encoded in language to the most grievous sort. That these encounters are experienced by a child gives this story an uncommon power.

With slow, intentional, sure-footed pacing, the troubles of the adult world seep into the child narrator's consciousness. Alive to every sound and sense, our young narrator draws the Southern world of her grandparents, her sensitivity heightened because she is a city girl come down for an extended visit while her mother recovers from personal turmoil. Yes, like many children, she is afraid of the dark—a fear that naturally contributes to the ominous suspense of the story.

"Looking out into the darkness," she says, "felt more like the darkness was looking into me." Over the course of the story, this darkness becomes a void that takes physical form in the white people at the margins of this story. The narrator's accutely embodied reception of her environment renews our sensitivity to the evils of the world. Lest we continue unaware of the voids inside us—whether caused by habitual and historical being or racial trauma—we'd best read fiction like Zkara Gaillard's "A Good Word"—which, I'd wager, will be studied in classrooms sometime soon and for years to come.

Tanya Larkin, Managing Editor
Transition Magazine

A Good Word

Zkara Gaillard

For Harry and Lula Mae Gaillard

WE KNEW SOMETHING WAS WRONG. GRAMMA HAD just sent us outside because we'd been making too much of a racket inside her house. Glad for permission, we didn't ask her why she had changed her mind. We put on our flip-flops and clambered out the back door to find Pop. The sun was high in the sky and crooked to one side like a drawing. We drank in the first bit of sun that we'd had all afternoon, the summer heat weighing down on us like a tight hug. The world outside was unnaturally quiet, like a held breath. The trees did not dance with the breeze, the birds were songless, and there was a stinging sharpness in the air. Something was wrong—we just didn't know what.

We had been at Gramma and Pop's house for weeks, and the excitement of being away from home was gone. Last night someone called the house. It was late, and we were sitting on the living room floor, eating butter-pecan ice cream in plastic cups. Gramma and Pop stood together by the landline, listening but not talking. When they hung up, Gramma sent us to bed without making sure we brushed our teeth. The rest of the night we could hear Pop and Gramma talk quietly in the living room. They were still sitting there in the morning. When Uriah had asked if we could go play outside, Gramma started hollering at him. We had spent most of the day letting the television whisper PBS documentaries to itself as we made up games to play on the cool floor of the living room.

We raced around the house to the driveway, finding Pop hunched over the hood of his burgundy van. He wore his stained lawn-mowing sneakers and a faded-brown bucket hat that he would swap out with his fishing hat or his church hat. Pop wiped his forehead and neck with a rag, leaning to pick up one of the bottles that littered the floor beside his toolbox. Pop was usually working on something. He liked to be outside from sunup to sundown, making repairs on things around the house I didn't even know needed fixing. Sometimes he would even fix things at other people's houses, and we loved when he took us along.

"Whatchu doin', Pop?" Moses called. He reached the van first, breathing heavily from beating us all. He had just turned twelve, and insisted on showing us the muscles and mustache that were apparently growing in. I couldn't see it.

Pop mumbled from under the hood, waving his hand.

"Huh?" Uriah grunted. He was just behind Moses at eleven, but he looked younger because he still hadn't hit his growth spurt.

Pop lifted his head. "Git me that wrench—the one with the yellow stripe."

Moriah reached the wrench first, handing it to Pop before joining our brothers to peek at his work. People always thought that Moriah and Uriah were twins because they were always the same height even though he was a year older than her. The only difference was Uriah's duck-footed walk, and Moriah's long hair was split into two cornrows.

Gramma and Pop's house was long but not tall, with red-brown bricks and a long driveway that curved toward the gravel road.

Although it was nice not to have to share two lumpy mattresses with my sisters and brothers like we did at our apartment back home, I was still homesick. I breathed in the air, taking in the trees around our grandparents' house. They looked like the same evergreen trees that we had back home, except they didn't smell the same. Ours were crisp, almost minty, in the colder air, but here they were warm and sappy. Maybe it was the sun, which got so hot down here that we'd spend whole days at church and be happy about it because there was AC.

It was the same hot sun that turned our gray-brown skin from the sunless northern winter to a ripe, dark baked brown every summer. Each time we came home to start school, Momma would kiss our faces, saying, "Look at my pretty brown babies." I missed Momma, probably more than anybody else. I wasn't sure why we were still here, I don't think any of us knew. Even Tamar was scared to ask when Pop was going to drive us back. Gramma talked about picking out school clothes soon, but we normally did that with Momma.

"Go an' git me somethin' to drink." Pop waved his dirty towel at Moses and ducked under the hood. Moses ran inside as the rest of us walked closer.

"Is somethin' wrong with the van?" Uriah asked.

Pop pointed at a yellow bottle at his feet. "No, just replacin' the fluids. Makin' sure everythin' is fine. Tamar, climb in there an' start it up for me."

Tamar slid into Pop's seat, buckling her seat belt like Pop taught her to. Pop had let us all sit in the driver's seat, pointing out the gas and the brake and the different gear shifts, but since Tamar was fourteen, she was the only one he allowed to circle the dirt roads around the house.

Moriah followed her and sat in Gramma's seat. I was right behind, until Uriah jumped in front of me, shoving me away from the door.

I tripped on my flip-flops and scuffed my hands against the pavement. Red pearls of blood blossomed across my palms. I could feel my nose get hot and prickly. My lips trembled and I breathed heavily to keep the tears back. Still, they escaped. I wiped at them with my stinging hands.

Uriah frowned at me. "You're such a baby."

I struggled to stand, choking back the sobs that marked me the baby. I was eight. I was the youngest, the shortest, the weakest. I didn't get to have what I wanted.

"No, I'm not." But my voice wobbled.

I hated the word. *Baby.* It wasn't a bad word, really. Nothing like the swear words that made Momma pop us, even though she said them all the time. Something about the way the bad words tingled on our tongues when we whispered insults at each other behind Momma's back, or screamed them out into the bright chaos of the city beyond our windows at night, made us risk having our mouths washed out with soap. No, *baby* wasn't a bad word. Momma called us hers, and even Moses was happy to be her baby. Still, it wasn't a good word. The way they said it was like a bad thing. It was something wrong, something I couldn't change about myself no matter how hard I tried.

Uriah ignored me, squeezing beside Moriah and closing the door so that I couldn't see what they were doing. I stood, pulling open the back door and sliding into the middle bucket seat I never got to sit in. The van smelled like Gramma's strong perfume, the one she wore when we went to church, flowery and light. I smiled to myself, feeling like a pilot or a captain. It amazed me that the boys got to feel like this all the time. On the mirror, a wooden cross hung on a piece of fuzzy twine. The cross looked hand-carved. It had been there for as long as I could remember. Pop signaled for Tamar to start the car. She put her foot on the brake as she turned the key. The van rumbled underneath us.

"Check the air," Pop called. He drank deeply from a can of Cheerwine that Moses had brought out. Moriah leaned over to press the button. First it felt like hot breath coming through the vents, but the longer it ran, the cooler it got. We cheered as he closed the hood.

"Time to go." Gramma came outside and locked the door behind her. She had changed into a long, yellow, flowery dress like all the other dresses she wore every day.

We knew better than to ask where we were headed. Instead, we climbed into our own seats. Moses and Uriah sat in the middle row. I sat in the back row, between Tamar and Moriah, far from any of the windows and just missing the weak spurts of cool air. Gramma turned up the music, and the deep voice of a woman filled the van. I couldn't understand the words that she was saying—if she was saying any words at all—but I could tell she was sad. I watched the brown cross swing back and forth in the window. I always found comfort in that brown cross. My eyes would rest on it whenever we would drive anywhere, watching it swing patiently from side to side. Dark clouds started to gather in the sky.

The one thing I hated about Gramma and Pop's house was the dark. Back home there wasn't anything like pure darkness. There was always some sort of light: a streetlight, a car, an ambulance, the buildings all around us. There were always people too. It didn't matter what time it was, there was a person on the street. I liked how it was never really night. I could always see, a voice was never far. Looking out into the night was a comfort. Down here, it really became night. After the sunset, I couldn't see anything but the moon. The only sounds were the crickets and cicadas and, if I were up late enough, animals hunting. But never any people. Looking out into the darkness felt more like the darkness was looking into me.

WE FINALLY PULLED up in front of a wide blue house with a palmetto tree growing in the front lawn. The overgrown garden almost completely covered the lawn ornaments—frogs, butterflies, mushrooms, snails. Tamar groaned, but we were all feeling the same way. It was Mrs. Rudine's house. The only good thing about coming to Mrs. Rudine's house was that she had AC and she let us feed the chickens, but that was about it. Parked in the driveway were two trucks: her husband's red truck and a silver one. It was Uncle Ant's, Momma's little brother. We got out of the van and waited on the porch while Pop rang the doorbell. Moriah kicked at one of the metal frogs wearing a top hat, but it popped back up.

When Mr. Earl answered the door, he let us in without saying anything. He didn't usually talk unless he had to. Mrs. Rudine was Aunt Sandra's mom, and when Aunt Sandra married our uncle Ant, she became kinda related to us. Gramma reminded us to call Rudine "Mrs." and not "Aunt" when I accidentally did once. We came to their house the least out of all our family. Mrs. Rudine was waiting in the living room. She was a short woman, with hair pressed flat and into big lion curls.

"Hey, it's good to see y'all." Mrs. Rudine hugged Pop and Gramma and then turned to us. We each gave her a hug, but none of us wanted to. She smelled like baby powder even though she didn't have a baby.

"Hey, y'all," Aunt Sandra called from the kitchen. She was my favorite aunt out of all our aunts, great-aunts included. She was really pretty, with long hair that she would sometimes let us braid. Momma didn't really do girly stuff with us, so when Uncle Ant and Aunt Sandra would come up to visit, she would have sleepovers with us to teach us how to paint our nails and find out our skin's undertones. We all ran to hug her, but I held on extra long.

"How are y'all holdin' up?" Gramma asked.

Mrs. Rudine waved her hand, slapping the question out of the air.

"We're fine." Aunt Sandra shot a glance over at us. "Do the kids—"

"No, we didn't tell them nothin'," Gramma said quickly, with a sharp look on her face.

"Where's Anthony?" Pop asked her.

"Daddy left him out back," Aunt Sandra answered, finally pulling away from me with a kiss on top of my head.

"Lemme show you what I got goin' on back there," Mr. Earl said to Pop as they walked out the back door.

Gramma pointed to a tall blue-and-white vase that came up to her hip and asked Mrs. Rudine where she got it, even though Gramma had her own collection of blue and white dishes at our house. Mrs. Rudine's house wasn't very big, we could pretty much see the whole thing from the front entrance. The living room and dining room in front, the kitchen to the right, the bedrooms to the left. We had lost our chance to go outside when Pop left, and we weren't sure if we needed permission to leave. We looked at Tamar silently for directions. She shrugged and sat down on the couch, the same blue as the house, still covered in plastic. The cushions chafed and crumpled as the rest of us sat down. The AC was up so high that it didn't take long for us to start shivering.

"Ask if we can turn the TV on," Moses whispered to Tamar.

"Ask if we can go outside." Moriah picked at the seam of the plastic covering.

"Ask if we can turn the AC down." Uriah put his arms into his shirt and hugged himself.

"Yah go ask," Tamar hissed back.

"Do y'all kids want somethin' to eat?" Mrs. Rudine asked us. "I got a pot of black-eyed peas on the stove."

Not sure if we were allowed to accept food from her, we looked to Gramma.

Gramma shook her head. "We're not stayin' long, an' I don't wanna put you outta your way."

Mrs. Rudine sucked her teeth. "They can have a cookie, at least."

We looked at Gramma again. She nodded with a small smile, and Mrs. Rudine waved us into the kitchen with her hand. The plastic stuck to our legs a little when we stood.

In the kitchen, Mrs. Rudine pointed to a big tan glass jar on the counter, with a brown bear hugging it. My brothers and sisters picked a cookie from the top and thanked her quickly to go back and sit down. I was the last to pick out my cookie, and when I saw that there were different choices inside, I tried to dig for the one I wanted. Mrs. Rudine watched me search.

"It's real good of y'all to take these kids offa Diane." I looked at Gramma and saw that her face was screwed up. I could tell she wanted to say something back.

"Tamar," Gramma called out. My sister came back through the doorway. "Y'all can go on outside an' feed the chickens. Make sure it's okay with Mrs. Rudine."

"May we go and feed the chickens, ma'am?" Tamar asked.

Mrs. Rudine nodded. "Y'all know where the feed is at."

My hand stopped in the jar. I thought that if I didn't move, they would forget that I was in the kitchen with them.

"Rhoda, this is grown folks' talk." Gramma turned to me. "Go on."

"Yes, ma'am." I grabbed the cookie I had my hand on and put the lid back on the jar. I walked slowly to the back door, trying to think of a way to stay inside the house. I stood in the living room, but they were quiet. I walked to the storm door, pushed it open, and let it slam against the frame. Then crouched by the wall that blocked the kitchen from the living room.

"You better than me, raisin' kids twice," Mrs. Rudine scoffed like she had heard a bad joke. "Least they ain't babies."

"We're happy to look after 'em till Diane gets back on her feet." Gramma sounded strange, like she was faking a smile.

"The minute that good-for-nothin' husband of hers left, she shoulda came back down. If it had been Sandra in that situation, me an' Earl woulda went an' dragged her back here, if that's what it took."

"Ma!" Aunt Sandra sounded embarrassed.

"I'm just sayin', she shit the bed, let the girl lie in it."

"I hear you," Gramma said. "But what's done is done."

They all were quiet for a moment. I looked at the cookie in my hand—oatmeal raisin—and waited for them to say more. They were so quiet that I thought they could hear me breathing. I don't think Gramma had ever been so quiet. Maybe she didn't like Mrs. Rudine either. I was about to go outside when I heard Aunt Sandra.

"Ant won't talk to me about what happened. He don't want me to be scared, but I think not knowin' is scarier than anythin' else."

"Did they find out who it was?" Mrs. Rudine asked.

Gramma cleared her throat. "It was Geenah Collins's boy."

The AC rumbled so loudly I almost couldn't hear what they were saying. I moved closer to the kitchen door. The light of the kitchen shined a rectangle of brightness into the dark living room. I made sure not to step in the light.

"Tyson?"

"No, the younger one, Darnell."

"Ant and Darnell played football together in high school," Aunt Sandra whispered. "That's his friend."

"Mm-mm-mm," Mrs. Rudine groaned.

"What happened?" Aunt Sandra asked.

Gramma kept talking. "He been workin' at the Coke plant wit' some white boys. Guess he thought they was friends an' all, went drinking wit' 'em at the bar down aways."

"Musta said somethin' them white boys didn't like," Mrs. Rudine muttered under her breath.

"Don't take nothin' but a change in the breeze to set 'em off." Gramma sounded annoyed. "You know that."

"You right," Aunt Sandra said. "Then what?"

"They strung that boy up. Tied his arms to a tree. Beat him to death's door. Cut his face up." Gramma sighed. "He couldn't open his eyes, let alone say his own name."

Goose bumps moved from my arms, spread down my back, and went through my legs.

Mrs. Rudine made a noise in the back of her throat. "A damn shame."

"Who found him?" Aunt Sandra asked.

"Maggie's grandson. They dropped him in the yard, rope still round his neck."

"Lordamercy," Aunt Sandra gasped. "The poor baby."

"She's the one who called us. Henry wouldn't sleep, he just sat there wit' the gun all night."

"What did you do?" Mrs. Rudine asked.

"I stayed wit' him the whole night." Gramma scoffed. "Tried to keep the kids in, but you know how they git."

". . . don't listen to nobody." Aunt Sandra chuckled a little.

"Ain't been a lynchin' here in least a decade. Why now?" I wasn't sure if Gramma really wanted an answer.

Mrs. Rudine clicked her teeth in disagreement.

"If *lynchin'* ain't a good word for it, then what is?" Gramma asked.

"I don't know, but that's a strong word for it."

"It's the *only* word for it," Gramma said.

The frosting on the cookie was sticky on my fingers. I felt sick. I wanted to throw the cookie away, but I didn't want to go back into the kitchen. I heard Aunt Sandra start another question, but I didn't want to hear any more. I stood and walked through the storm door, placing it back gently. The yard wasn't as overgrown as the front, but still longer than Pop kept it at our house. The chicken coop was on one side and the shed was on the other. There wasn't a fence or anything blocking off the woods that started behind their house. I found my brothers and sisters next to the chicken coop.

"You gonna eat that?" Moses asked when I walked up beside him. I shook my head and gave him the cookie. I wiped my clammy hands against my jeans.

The chickens clucked excitedly, racing to eat the feed that Moriah and Tamar had sprinkled on the ground. Uriah danced around the fence, making silly noises as if he could talk to them. I tried to laugh along with them, opening my mouth and closing it again. I thought about whether I should tell them what I heard. Maybe not everyone, maybe just Tamar. She would know what to do.

"Tamar," I called out to her.

"Yeah?" Tamar glanced up at me for a second, but then she pointed her finger to the other side of the yard.

We turned around and saw Pop, Uncle Ant, and Mr. Earl standing over something in the woods behind the house. My brothers sprinted over, and the rest of us were close behind them. Within a few feet we could see what it was.

It was a deer. They had hung it from the branches of the tree with a bunch of rope. Its top legs were tied back, and its head lay limp to the side like its neck was broken. The eyes were big and brown and lifeless. I didn't like how human its eyes were. I didn't like how much different than human eyes they were. Even with the heat, goose bumps raised on my arms. I looked away. I could see patches of lavender sky between the leafy branches of the trees. It seemed darker than it was before as we stood in front of the dead animal.

"Did you shoot it?" I asked. My brothers walked to get a better look.

Mr. Earl took a knife from his leather belt and pointed with it. "The leg's broke."

"Then what happened?" Moses asked. "Why's it dead?"

"Car hit it an' left it in the road." Mr. Earl answered as if he hadn't ever heard a stupider question.

Moriah took a step back. "Why is it in the yard, though?" Mr. Earl didn't answer.

"It's offseason," Uncle Ant said, then grunted as he bent and laid out pieces of blue tarp beneath the animal. He stood and straightened his baseball cap. "It's illegal to kill a deer right now."

Without any warning, Mr. Earl placed his knife at the bottom of the deer and ran it all the way up its body. Pop and Uncle Ant helped hold the deer's lower legs in place as he made the cuts. We all stood in silent horror as Mr. Earl reached his hands inside and started to pull things out.

"No use in wastin' good meat."

First it was the smell. Thick and coppery. I coughed on it like a mouthful of pennies. Then the stomach fell out, and with it came the corn, grass, and nuts that the deer must've last eaten. It smelled nasty and woodsy and sweet at the same time. Mr. Earl kept pulling stuff out. It all landed on the tarp with soft plopping sounds. I looked back into the eyes of the deer. Big and brown. Empty. Flat. Every time Mr. Earl touched it, I swear I saw it flinch. And even though I knew it couldn't be true, I felt like it was still alive somehow, that it was in pain.

"A'right." Mr. Earl stood and wiped the back of his hand against his sweaty face, leaving a red mark across his forehead. I stared down at the pile of the deer's insides and wondered how big a pile of my own insides would be if somebody was to cut me open.

"I'll pull the truck around." Uncle Ant walked off to the front of the house. Pop and Mr. Earl gathered the tarps. After dumping it in some bags, they walked to the hose at the side of the house to rinse off their knives. We stood looking at the deer, its entire body opened up and hollowed out. My stomach felt funny.

Moses crept closer to the deer, reaching out a finger to touch it. "Dare me?"

"Stop it," Tamar said.

"You're all punks." Moses poked the deer. He walked around the tree, making faces like he was scared as he went. He picked up a twig and weighed it in his hand.

"What do you call a deer with no eyes?" He pointed the stick at each of us as he waited for an answer.

"Moses, I'm gonna go tell Pop and Gramma if you don't stop," Tamar warned, but her voice shook.

Moses stabbed the stick through the deer's eye. The eye burst, and this thick bloody stuff came running down the deer's neck. He laughed and stabbed the other eye. My nose prickled and my eyes got hot.

"I have no eye-deer." Moses spun around to face us and continued laughing.

"Moses!" Tamar yelled uselessly.

Moriah bent over and threw up onto the grass. I could see the cookies she ate, tan and gritty, and bits of brown that could have been the fried bologna sandwiches we'd had at lunch. Uriah spit on the ground a couple times and chewed the inside of his cheeks to keep his mouth closed. He looked just as sick as Moriah was. Tears came running down my face as I watched the deer's hollowed-out eyes drip into the grass.

"Rhoda, you stay cryin' about somethin'." Moses threw the stick in front of me. "Shit. It's not all that."

I jumped back as it landed and bumped into Pop.

"Don't make me wash your mouth out wit' soap, boy," Pop snapped.

"Sorry, sorry." Moses kicked at the bloody stick.

Pop turned to look at us. "What's goin' on?"

"Nothin'," Moses said quickly. The rest of us didn't answer.

Pop squinted at the deer. The dark-blue storm clouds growing over half the sky made it hard to see the difference between the bloody trails left by Mr. Earl and Moses.

"Can I help?" Moses stepped in between Pop and the deer.

"Watch it." Pop nodded to the side.

We moved out of the way as Mr. Earl walked backward across the lawn directing Uncle Ant, who was backing the truck as close to the trees as he could get it.

Uncle Ant hopped out of the truck, and they got back to work. Pop grabbed hold of the deer's legs as Uncle Ant and Mr. Earl cut it down from the tree. Once Mr. Earl put his knife back on his belt, they lifted the deer off the ground and into the tarp-covered bed of the truck. Moriah gagged again as the deer's body thudded against the metal.

"Why didn't you say you was feeling sick?" Gramma asked, grabbing Moriah before she fell over. Aunt Sandra was right behind her. Mrs. Rudine was coming down the back steps behind them, a wicker basket in her arm with a towel covering what was inside. Pop and Mr. Earl wrapped the deer with rope.

"A bunch of city kids," Mrs. Rudine tut-tutted at us. "Probably never seen somethin' like this."

Tamar frowned at her but didn't say anything. Uriah spit on the ground again.

Aunt Sandra walked over and gave me a hug. "Are y'all okay?"

I nodded with my body pressed against hers, squeezing her even when she tried to pull away. She gave me a squeeze back and left her arms around me. The sun had finally set, but the sky was still a deep purple. The only light in the yard came from the headlights of Mr. Earl's truck and the dim yellow floodlight above the back door. The air was heavy, and the skin of my cheek was sticky against Aunt Sandra's arm.

"A'right. I think we should get these kids home," Gramma said.

Pop held out the garden hose so Mr. Earl and Uncle Ant could clean the blood off their hands, then he washed his own hands one after the other.

Mrs. Rudine looked down at Moriah. "She don't look like she gon' be standin' up much longer."

"Quit that spittin' an' help your sister," Gramma called to Uriah. She passed Moriah to him and Tamar. The three of them made their way to the van.

"Gramma, can we ride in the back of Uncle Ant's truck?" Moses pleaded.

"No, it's too dark for that. I don't want y'all tumblin' out an' fallin' into a ditch." Gramma shook her head. "Go on."

I didn't want to let go of my aunt yet. I hadn't had a hug this long since we were home. The last hug Momma had given us, there had been tears on her face. "May I ride with Aunt Sandra and Uncle Ant?"

Moses sucked his teeth. "That's not fair."

"What did I say? Go on." Gramma swatted at him, then looked at Aunt Sandra.

She nodded. "There's space for her. We'll be right behind you."

"Behave. Listen to your aunt an' uncle," Gramma warned. I promised her I would.

Mrs. Rudine handed Gramma the basket in her hand. Something inside it rattled like small pieces of metal. "Here are some eggs an' the other thing you needed."

"Thank you—all we got is buckshot back home." Gramma smiled at her.

Mrs. Rudine chuckled. "That'd get the job done."

"It sure would." Pop nodded at her. "Have a good night."

"Call me when y'all get in. Drive safe." Mrs. Rudine waved to them as they piled into the van. It was weird watching it pull off. Either I was inside with my brothers and sisters or outside it with them. Never by myself.

"Earl got everything set up with a butcher, so I guess we can head off," Uncle Ant said as Mr. Earl drove away. The yard grew darker without his headlights.

"Before y'all leave, wait till I git you some protection." Mrs. Rudine turned to the house.

"Ma, we'll be fine," Aunt Sandra called to her. "We don't need anythin'."

But Mrs. Rudine was already back with something in her hand. "Can't have you walkin' round wit' nothin'. It's the only one I can give you for right now."

"Ma . . . ," Aunt Sandra complained as Mrs. Rudine handed it to Uncle Ant.

"I don't know why you so damn hardheaded. You're too grown not to know how to shoot." Mrs. Rudine kissed her teeth and looked at my uncle.

Uncle Ant turned it over in his hand. I squinted at it in the dim light and realized it was a gun. I had never seen a real gun before. Only in cartoons, long sticks that could be bent like a twig or exploded out the end like a bomb. But what he had seemed more real. Heavy. Solid. I let Aunt Sandra go and took a step behind her.

"Can you handle it?" Mrs. Rudine asked.

"Yes, ma'am. Pop taught me to shoot when I was a boy." He pressed something down on it, and a part jumped into his other hand. He put the pieces back together. His hands looked dark in places, but I couldn't tell if he had gotten all the blood off or if it was just the light. It looked like he knew what he was doing. Mrs. Rudine seemed to think so, too, nodding as she watched him. Aunt Sandra didn't look very happy, but she kept quiet.

"Goodnight, Ma." Aunt Sandra slid into the truck last. She and Uncle Ant were on either side of me. Uncle Ant passed her the gun, and she quickly opened the glove box, tucked the gun inside, and slammed it shut. She shook her hands like she had been burned. I laughed a little but stopped when I saw the look on her face. Mrs. Rudine stood at the front door, but she didn't wave. Uncle Ant honked his horn as we drove out onto the road.

Night had come by the time we left Mrs. Rudine's. The sky was so much bigger down here, it just went on for miles and miles. It felt like once night came, it swallowed the whole world in its pitch black. There was no real escape except to wait for the morning sun, but that was hours away. The truck's headlights carved a narrow path of sight, but it wasn't enough to chase away the shadow that everything had become. I shrank into my seat a little. Whatever was in the darkness that I couldn't see could still see me.

Music filled the truck as I touched one of Aunt Sandra's braids. "I wish my hair was as pretty as yours."

She smiled at me. "Your hair is very pretty."

"Hey, what about me?" Uncle Ant asked.

I tried to think of what was under the cap he always wore. "You don't have hair."

"I don't have hair?" He threw his cap off and pointed to his cropped hair. "What's all this?"

"Yeah, you're bald." I started giggling at the wild look on his face.

"Bald?" He shoved his cap back on.

Aunt Sandra put her arms around me as we laughed. "I can show you how to do it yourself."

"Really?"

"Yeah, maybe I can stay tonight. We'll see what your grandparents say when we get back, okay?"

"Can you teach me to do my hair like y—"

"Hold on," Uncle Ant shushed us and turned the music down. A rattling sound filled the cab. He jerked the truck to the side of the road and stomped on the brake.

"Fuck."

I had never heard Uncle Ant say a bad word before.

Aunt Sandra put her hand out to touch his. "What's wrong?"

"We need gas." He rubbed his hand across his face, knocking his cap crooked. "I didn't think that we was gonna be out today. Thought I'd be able to get some before work tomorrow."

Aunt Sandra didn't say anything, but her eyes got big. I had never thought about what would happen if a car ran out of gas. I assumed it would still drive, maybe slower, but drive until they could eventually get more. Like when the AC in Pop's van could only push out hot air until he put more fluid inside. The car's headlights shined into the woods on the side of the road. The light wasn't bright enough to see very far into the trees. Something could be out there, just outside of the light, watching us.

Uncle Ant started talking really fast. "I'm gonna need to make a run. There's a station a mile or two up this way. I'll be fastest alone. I can leave y'all in here—"

"I am not lettin' you go out there by yourself." Aunt Sandra shook her head. They just stared at each other for a moment. Then she looked down at me.

"She'll slow us down," Uncle Ant said before she even opened her mouth.

"Ant . . . ," Aunt Sandra stuttered but didn't say anything else.

"No one is gonna mess wit' a car on the side of the road. If she stays down, no one can see her. She's safer here than out there wit' us." I watched something pass between them as they looked at each other.

It took me a second to figure out that they were meaning to leave me in the truck by myself. Goose bumps raised on my arms. Uncle Ant grabbed my hand to get my attention.

"We're gonna get some gas. I need you to get low down in the seat an' stay quiet for me. I'm gonna knock like this." He rapped his knuckles against the window four times. "Don't get up till you hear this. If you see somethin', if you hear anythin' else but this, do not get up. Do you understand?"

I nodded, but I wasn't sure if I really understood.

Uncle Ant turned the truck off, and the music and headlights went with it. My heart thumped in my chest as my eyes grew used to the dark. He got out of the truck and started to search for something in the back. Aunt Sandra put her hand on the glove box but then pulled it away. We watched Uncle Ant make his way around the front of the truck, a large flashlight in one hand and a gas can in the other. I could barely see that he was standing there. My aunt opened the glove box and took the gun out. She held it funny, like it would jump out of her hand.

"We'll be right back." Aunt Sandra stepped out, stumbling a little on the uneven ground. "Lock both the doors."

I leaned over and pressed the locks down. Aunt Sandra walked to meet Uncle Ant in front of the truck. They turned to me and started talking, but I couldn't hear what they said. Uncle Ant waved his hand up and down. He kept doing it until I realized he wanted me to get down. I ducked, lying curled up in the seat. I didn't like not being able to see them walk away. I didn't know when I was finally alone. My heartbeat thudded in my ears. It was the only thing I could hear other than my panting breath. I looked up, searching for the wooden cross. But I remembered that it was in Pop's van with the rest of my brothers and sisters. Where I should have been. It would have been nice to have it.

It was so quiet my ears strained trying to catch anything. Noises beyond the sound of my own breath sent my heart thudding wildly in my chest, drowning everything out. I wished I could hear Momma sing again. She thought she had a bad voice, so she tried not to very often. But when Momma was tired, she would sing this song to herself, she didn't seem to realize it. It was the same thing over and over, I have never heard her sing the rest of the words. *Nobody knows the trouble I've seen, nobody knows but Jesus. Nobody knows the sorrows I've had, no one knows but Him.* I thought the words in my head, but when that felt like it wasn't enough, I sang the song out loud, repeating the words.

DARKNESS ATE EVERYTHING, stealing any feeling of safety the truck had given me. Locked doors don't keep the night out. My whole body shivered as I realized that this was the first time I'd ever been all alone. The air inside the cabin had become damp from my panting breaths and the growing humidity. A part of me knew that my mind was playing tricks on me, but that did not stop my building panic. My eyes searched for anything to hold on to. I shut them. My ears searched for sounds that weren't there. I sang Momma's song louder, but hearing the tremor in my voice made me even more scared. My voice alone couldn't chase away the darkness.

A wave of light washed over my shut eyes, lighting up the truck like a spotlight. I opened my eyes, greedily taking in the sight that the light gave me. I tried to see if there was someone out there, but all I could see from where I lay was the pitch-black sky. I stayed where I was, remembering I needed to wait for my uncle's signal. Yet I couldn't help but feel calmer now that it was bright again. Light chased away the darkness. Light meant I was safe. I stopped singing, my heart slowing as I waited for my aunt and uncle to return to the car. It did not occur to me that the light could have been anything other than Uncle Ant's flashlight.

Sharp banging on the car window startled me up out of my

seat. A deep, cold fear gripped me as I took in what was beyond the window. I noticed the eyes first. Black holes sunk into a chalky pale face pulled into a grotesque smile. Somewhere between human and not. The white man on the other side just stood there as we stared at each other. Then, as if possessed by some sudden rage, the man began to slam his fleshy hands against the window. He grabbed the door handle and pulled on it, rattling so hard it seemed seconds away from breaking off the door. The pale man's grunts leached through the locked door, the only thing separating his hands from reaching me. The entire truck shook with his fists. But I just stared at him, heart hammering in my chest. No matter how hard he hit the window, I didn't do anything but stare. I was stuck, terrified of what would happen when he finally got through the door. I imagined my insides in a pile on the floor.

Just as suddenly as he started, he stopped.

"It's just a pickaninny."

The white man's voice was softer than I thought it would be, muffled, but not enough to make me feel safe from his words. They moved slowly, the words leaving the heavy feeling of damp static on my skin. The pale man slammed his hand one last time with a sharp crack. Fear froze me stiff as I watched him turn away from the truck as if he was disappointed. He staggered back toward the car with two other white men. I continued to stare out the window. My sight left me as the headlights disappeared into the night.

I stared into the flat dark beyond the hood of the truck, waiting for my eyes to pick up something, anything. I don't know how long I sat there like that, watching the unmoving blackness. It went on forever. I wasn't sure at first, but I realized that I could make out Aunt Sandra and Uncle Ant running along the side of the road. They were hunched over as if they were one sound away from jumping to hide in the woods. I watched them run to the side of the truck. Aunt Sandra waited as Uncle Ant lifted the gas can to fill the truck up. When he was done, he tossed the can in the back and unlocked the door. As he climbed in, I saw that the gun was tucked in his belt.

"I told you to stay down until I knocked." Uncle Ant leaned over me to unlock the door for Aunt Sandra, who slid in and slammed the door behind her. He lifted his hand from the seat. "Jesus, she wet herself."

He grabbed my shoulder, shaking me as he spoke. "What happened? Did somethin' happen? Did you see somebody?"

"Anthony, the child is scared," Aunt Sandra said sharply. She pulled at his hand until he let go. "Shit, I'm scared."

Uncle Ant pushed a breath out roughly and started the car. I couldn't see anything past the headlights on the empty road ahead of us.

"Did you see anythin', baby?" Aunt Sandra asked.

I shook my head. What I had seen didn't seem real to me. It barely does now. It was like I had lost my words. The pale face in the darkness had taken them from me. Emptied out into its hollow eyes. She rubbed my back but it didn't bring the same comfort.

"What was you and Donny talkin' about at the station?"

Uncle Ant rubbed his jaw, stuttering a little over his words. "He said that some white folks bought that house bein' built down near my parents."

She frowned at him. "No, I heard that. He said somethin' else to you."

He pressed his lips together and pushed a sigh out his nose. Aunt Sandra stayed quiet, waiting for his answer.

"Darnell died a couple of hours ago." She stared at him in silent horror, but Uncle Ant just kept going as if he was scared to stop talking. "I should go by his mother's house an' pay my respects. I hope Tyson don't get no stupid ideas about goin' after nobody, his mother's been through eno—"

"What's a pickaninny?"

It was so quiet in the car it sounded like they had both stopped breathing. Aunt Sandra looked at me, but I just stared at the road being eaten by the hood of the truck.

"It's not a good word," she whispered.

I watched the dark sky above the dark road in front of me. I thought of the eyes, hollow and lifeless. I could see the sweat that ran bloody out of gouged-out sockets. I waited for my nose to burn, for the tears to come. They never would. A roll of thunder shook the world around me. Lightning cracked across the sky, pitching the world into flashing brightness for less than a second. Another roll of thunder rattled the ribs in my chest. Another bolt of lightning streaked through the sky. It looked like a white hand coming out of the black expanse, reaching down to get me. The words of Momma's song ran through my head. They weren't good enough words for me.

Zkara Gaillard was born in South Carolina and raised in Schenectady, New York. They earned their BA in English from the University of South Carolina and their MFA in fiction from the Iowa Writers' Workshop, alongside a graduate certificate in African American studies. They live in New York City.

Editor's Note

Leanne Ma's "Guilty Parties" is a collective exploration of personal responsibility—to our friendships, our families, our cultures and countries, and especially to ourselves and our own ideals. Guided by the communal voice of four young girls as they grow up in a rapidly changing Hong Kong, the reader is invited to join the "we" of the tight group of friends as they look on in judgment, distaste, and, ultimately, awe at the errant fifth member of their squad, the audacious and rebellious Natalie. When Natalie's prodemocratic associations and actions land her in prison amid hostility from an increasingly authoritative Chinese government, all five girls, now women, are left to reconcile with what it really means to be free. For a story with so much turmoil—both public and personal—the writing is confident and firm, even as the world depicted becomes more and more unsteady. In "Guilty Parties," Leanne Ma cleverly homes in on the most interesting aspect of moral certainty: its blurry, vulnerable boundaries.

Katie Sticca, Managing Editor
Salamander

Guilty Parties

Leanne Ma

EVERY MONDAY MORNING BEFORE SCHOOL, WE AS-sembled in class lines in the covered playground, from shortest to tallest. On the first day of second grade, we were the four shortest girls in class: Angie, Bernadette, Clara, and Denise. A large rickety fan whirred above the principal's head on the lectern as she delivered morning announcements, but we were too short to feel the breeze. Beyond the iron gate, a double-decker bus rumbled down Bonham Road, shaking the cement beneath our snug Mary Janes. Flapping our sticky white qipao-style uniform dresses to cool our blazing bodies, we swallowed saliva to quench our dry throats, impatient to chant the only words we knew to the school song: *Glory! Glory! Saint Theresa's girls live forever!*

But when the announcements ended, the school song did not play. Instead, four tall upper-grade girls marched up to the front of the playground, two of them with long flags tucked under their armpits. Working in pairs, they hooked the flags onto the two poles next to the lectern. An unfamiliar tune started playing, and the flags were thrust into the air, unfurling the five-star red flag of China and the red-white bauhinia-flower flag of Hong Kong. The flags were hoisted up at the same time, slowly, and by the last note of the song, they reached the top of the pole, blowing robustly in the fan's current.

It was the most solemn event we'd ever witnessed. We wondered when we would grow tall enough to hoist the flags ourselves. What was the meaning of this new ceremony? We looked quizzically at each other. We couldn't remember. Everything was different in the second grade.

"We were a British colony," a voice behind us said. Natalie—we later learned her name—had a chubby face, dark bushy brows, and large thoughtful eyes. Her hair was tightly wound into pigtails tied with pink ribbons. "We were given back to China on July first."

"No, we weren't," we said, though we didn't know why. Maybe because we didn't like that she used a big word—*colony*—that we didn't understand. Maybe we didn't like to think that we were *given back* to anybody. Maybe we didn't like to think that Natalie, who was the fifth shortest in class, sounded like a self-righteous adult and knew something we didn't.

Finally, the school song started playing.

"Yes, we were. For ninety-nine years. My father told me." A blush lit up on her cheeks like a light bulb, as though she needed energy to power through her shyness. Why didn't she just keep her thoughts to herself? We didn't understand how long ninety-nine years was. What came after ninety-nine? We forgot, but we weren't going to ask the new girl. Instead, we said, in a voice mimicking her self-satisfaction, "You're not allowed to wear pink ribbons in your hair. Red or black plastic ties only."

Just then, one of the student monitors came over and pulled the five of us out of line. She marched us across the playground, past the lectern, in front of the entire assembly of watchful eyes as the loudspeakers belted out, *Glory! Glory!*

In the musty classroom, we were written up for detention and told to write "I will not chat during school assembly" one hundred times. One hundred, that's what came after ninety-nine.

When we finished copying out the lines, the student monitor supervising us was outside in the hallway. We swung our feet under the desks and looked at each other. We couldn't be more different: we had long and short hair, dark and porcelain skin, single and double eyelids, round gold-rimmed glasses and perfect vision, flat and tall noses, baby and adult teeth. But the ache in our forearms, from pressing pencil to paper, pulsed with the same anger. It was all because of Natalie, who was still writing, her mouth twitching with concentration. Her white school-uniform dress was so big that the chest had sunk to her waist, and her red tie looked like it had been pulled from her father's closet. The student monitor had given her a warning slip for the pink ribbons, and she'd taken them off. Untied hair was not allowed, but the yellow rubber bands tying up her hair, which she'd picked up off the classroom floor, still broke the rules. We wanted to be mad at her, but we also wanted to laugh. A girl like that couldn't be taken seriously.

"What does your father do?" we asked.

"He's a businessman."

We exchanged wary glances. Our fathers were also businessmen. They made men's undergarments, carpets, stereos, and watches in Chinese factories, packaged them in Hong Kong, and shipped them off to the world. What if Natalie's father made nicer watches or better underwear? Would our fathers lose their jobs? We would hate to become poor and have to work as cashiers at the ParknShop supermarket, which seemed to be the moral of every cautionary tale told by our parents: *make money or else.*

"What does he make?"

"He makes teddy bears."

Threat averted; we chuckled, wondering what the teddy bears looked like. We imagined snuggling up to the fuzzy belly of a giant Winnie-the-Pooh or Paddington Bear, or throwing tea parties in our bedrooms for small honey-brown bears on checkered picnic blankets with caramel popcorn.

From that moment on, we welcomed Natalie to our group. Her rough edges could be pieced into our puzzle: we had extra uniform dresses that fit, a new bag of red plastic hairbands, a generosity for the less fortunate. She was our missing piece. We told ourselves we wanted to understand what a "colony" was.

Who were we kidding? We wanted a free teddy bear.

FROM THAT DAY on, we took it upon ourselves to keep Natalie, the wild card, in check. We bribed student monitors with woven bracelets and chocolate bars, told every teacher they were our favorite, signed ourselves and Natalie up for the flag-raising roster the year we became old enough, believing that by being extra good, we could overcompensate for any of Natalie's potential missteps. Not that Natalie turned out to be much of a troublemaker—she eventually figured out the hair ties and wasn't even the most likely among us to be caught talking in class. In fact, in our group, she seemed to be more of a listener, a follower. But we liked to think that she needed us, and we liked being needed.

It shamed us to admit that the only time that need was asked of us, we failed to offer it. In our sixth-grade class, Natalie waved a thin sheet of Chinese calligraphy paper in the air and said, "I don't understand why we still have to do this stupid exercise from ancient times. Sometimes I just do it Sunday night before bed and get a B+, and other times I spend hours and get a B-. What's the difference between a B+ and B- in calligraphy? How is this making us better people?" She was looking directly at us, but we all knew she wasn't speaking to us.

Mrs. Chow put her hand on her pregnant belly, preparing her little one for the coming storm. She ordered Natalie to stand at the front of the class with her face against the blackboard. Mrs. Chow also looked straight at us, as though she and Natalie were incapable of communicating directly with each other.

Mrs. Chow turned to the blackboard and wrote *Benefits of Calligraphy* in large letters, underlining it with such force the piece of chalk snapped into two. We tried not to stare at Natalie and the ponytail sprouting from the back of her head. We thought Mrs. Chow would tell her to return to her seat after a while, or Natalie would faint or something and that would teach the teacher a lesson. But Mrs. Chow held tight to her pride and Natalie's spine held straight, so straight the chalky words appeared crooked on the board.

Soon the blackboard was filled with benefits: *Culture. Tradition. History. Art. Mind-body coordination. Cultivation of temperament. Builds character. Respect from others. Honor/Responsibility as Chinese.* With each word scrawled squeakily on the board, we felt more humiliated for Natalie, but the humiliation was also ours, because we were too scared to say something, anything. Had we spoken up, at least she wouldn't be standing up there all alone.

When the bell finally rang and Mrs. Chow said Natalie could go, we looked at each other, our armpits damp, as if we had been the ones standing for an hour. Natalie walked away from the blackboard and out the classroom door with her head held high, as if she had just completed her flag-raising duty. Not once did she look back at us—we weren't needed anymore. On the blackboard, we could see the spot where her nose tip had smudged against the chalk, and the cloud shape of her breath, spreading moist and dark against the green like mold. Too spent to chase her, we remained in our seats until Mrs. Chow ordered us to wipe the board clean before the next class.

Natalie was given detention and left off the flag-raising roster for three months. From then on, we learned that questions—though encouraged—were best kept to ourselves. And while spoken words stumbled and faltered, the quiet flicks of the calligraphy brush expressed honorable, unflappable character. *That* was the true lesson of calligraphy.

AFTER SIXTH GRADE, calligraphy became optional, but filing in class lines was not. Maybe the school was trying to instill in us a sense of discipline or camaraderie, or maybe it was the only way they knew how to manage people. Either way, the four of us were separated in the line—some of us moving up, others remaining near the front—but we were never far from each other.

Natalie hovered around the middle of the line throughout high school in height, but also in grades, in extracurriculars, in the number of boys from Saint Joseph's waiting for her outside the gate after school, in the number of Saint Theresa's girls who slipped love letters into her locker or scratched her name on the back of orange toilet doors. She had just the right disposition to avoid attention, jealousy, or threat, so much so that we soon forgot the way she had first barreled into our lives and how, like filing nails, we had rounded her jagged edges into conformity. The national anthem played weekly; nobody was paying attention anymore. The snack shop next to Saint Theresa's morphed into a tutoring center and then a Midland Realty by the time we graduated, while on the other side, the 7-Eleven stood steadfast over the years, its neon sign glowing brightly.

At the University of Hong Kong, we were no longer required to wear school uniforms and stand in lines. It was there that our paths diverged, where things began to go wrong. The four of us anchored ourselves to each other for the familiarity of the old and the comfort of established rules of group behavior, but the new environment signaled Natalie's break from us. She grew into something unrecognizable. We majored in finance, and Natalie in philosophy. We joined the Finance Club, while she joined the students' union, the Debating Society, the Political and Public Administration Association. We joked that, just to prove a point, she was probably causing trouble in the Calligraphy Society, too.

The university campus, carved out of a mountain slope, was a mix of Baroque-style red brick and granite buildings, flat-roofed structures with Shanghai plaster, and glossy new extension wings with green windows. We spent most of our days in the main library, studying for courses like Corporate Finance, the Economic System of Hong Kong, and China's Financial System and Markets. At first, Natalie tagged along, reading all the free newspapers on the rack and interrupting us with long-winded speeches. "When Hong Kong was given back to China, we all thought that over time, we were going to make China more like us, but the reality is that China is making us more like them," she would say.

"Well, we're failing at making you more like us, but if you don't shut up and let us study, you're going to be making us more like you," we said.

She gradually stopped coming to the library, and we saw less and less of her in person. And yet we didn't stop seeing her. Her headshot was everywhere, her bushy eyebrows peering down at us from the flyers and pamphlets pinned up on campus bulletins, championing some cause or event: *Tiananmen Square Student Vigil. July 1st March for Democracy. Symposium: Is China a Threat or Good for the World? Lunchtime Seminar Series: One Country, Two Systems: What's Next for Hong Kong?*

We met nice boys in our finance classes and constructed mental blueprints of beautiful homes on Bowen Road with beautiful children in them, paid for by beautiful salaries from Goldman Sachs. Meanwhile, Natalie met Alex and began destroying everything in her path, as if it was beneath her to want a stable, well-compensated life.

Alex Chan, visiting lecturer in Natalie's Public Policy, Politics, and Social Change class, was the chairman of the Hong Kong Social Democratic Party. When Alex was sixteen, his father was killed in a construction site accident. He quit school to set up a labor union to advocate for workers' rights, which later became the foundation for the party. A few years later, he volunteered to bring donations to the student protesters at Tiananmen Square, several days before the government crackdown. He survived, was arrested and detained for several days, then released back to Hong Kong after writing a letter of repentance. He was not allowed to return to China again. All this, we learned from Google. But growing up, he'd always been familiar to us as the bald T-shirt-wearing troublemaker in parliament, infamous for making headlines. Lugging an oakwood coffin into meetings to symbolize the death of democracy. Dangling handmade cloth marionettes over the speaker's desk to mock the puppet government. Hurling a plastic bag of dog shit across the chamber. Shouting, "Vindicate Tiananmen! End dictatorial rule! Fight for democracy!" and being carried out of chambers by security, feetfirst.

Soon after Alex visited Natalie's class, she began volunteering for him at his local councillor's office, opening letters from constituents and drafting replies for him. We thought it was just a phase, a line for her résumé, that this hot-blooded activism would eventually burn out and pass like a sharp rotten-egg fart. But when she started working there full-time after graduation, we couldn't decide which was worse: working for free for this lunatic or getting paid to become a lunatic herself.

Whenever Alex made the headlines for another of his antics, we couldn't help but picture Natalie sitting in her office—clicking through coffins online, untangling puppet strings, or running after some random dog at the park, scooping up fresh shit to fill plastic bags.

Gradually, one by one, we got married, talked about having babies, had babies, talked about our babies. Natalie came to all the bridal and baby showers and walked down the aisles in the chiffon bridesmaids' dresses politely, linking arms with each of the groomsmen chosen hopefully with her in mind. She behaved dutifully without complaint: sitting still as her lashes were curled, holding the bouquet at waist level with the peach roses facing outward, not rolling her eyes when she led guests to their tables. We almost expected her to launch into a political tirade at the end in exchange for her good behavior. But so rarely did she talk about her life—the life she had outside of us—that we were certain she was never *really* there with us, only physically.

We often wondered whether it was her politics that had led her down such an impractical path or if it had been her impractical study of the mind that had politicized her. We wondered whether there was anything that we could do or say to make her life easier, to make her more like us.

ONE DAY, PHOTOGRAPHS of Natalie and Alex appeared in the papers under the political-gossip column. They were sitting on metal folding chairs at a sidewalk stall, eating noodles under a green canopy. Her bob cut looked surprisingly good. Another paper showed them exiting his apartment together as the first rays of sunlight spilled onto the empty streets. Even in the pixelated image, the glow on her face was undeniable: they were sleeping together.

We read on. Alex was around fifty. A recent divorcé with two daughters. Sources "close to Natalie" said he'd stayed as long as he did in the marriage because of the kids; he'd relied on the wife to give them a sense of normalcy while he was working in politics to build a better future for Hong Kong. Our blood boiled again and again as we pored over the articles discussing our friend as if they knew her. Although we doubted the credibility of these "sources," we were stung with jealousy. Why had no one thought of interviewing us? We began dialing Natalie's number, but then thought of a better idea.

That same week, we marched into Alex's local councillor's

office. We were no longer small, but still we filed in shortest to tallest, orderly even by chance. At the front desk, we informed the secretary who'd asked for a name and appointment time that we were the Angry Victims of Hypocrisy, requiring an immediate appointment. Angie handed her a business card, and we headed straight for Alex's office. "But Mr. Chan is busy now!" she said. "You can't go in!"

Alex was on the phone, sitting at his desk. He looked up at us, amused, as though angry constituents and weak security were part of his routine. "I'll be with you in just a second," he whispered, hand over the receiver. We pulled over swivel chairs and sat down to wait, like silly school children in the teacher's office.

Alex had traded in his usual parliamentary uniform of T-shirt and jeans for a crisp, striped dress shirt and jeans, as though his work here, away from the cameras, deserved a modicum of decorum. He had dark skin and smelled nice: a light, warm cologne. He nodded into the phone, saying, "I understand your concern. I'll see what I can do."

His office was cluttered with pictures—of him, of his constituents and fellow democratic leaders, of rallies and protests and fundraisers—spanning years, decades of political life. At the center of the bookcase, embedded between thick, colorful book spines, was a framed picture of him at what appeared to be Tiananmen Square. He wore a white headband with a healthy amount of hair hanging over the sides. We almost didn't recognize him.

His desk was the only bare surface in the room. Apart from the computer and phone, there was only one picture on it—two baby girls smiling, eyes curved in slits like crescent moons, food dribbling over their faces—and no sign of his wife. We looked around the room again, searching for a picture of Natalie, but it was impossible to find her among the busy faces populating the shelves and walls. Disappointed, we let ourselves wonder for a moment if it would really be so bad for Natalie to be associated with this room, filled with history and gravitas like a cathedral hall. But then we shook off our awe, reprimanding ourselves for our lapse in reason, for succumbing to the romance of pursuing higher ideals. Wasn't being ourselves enough? We reached for each other's hands under the desk.

"So, what can I do for you?" Alex said, hanging up the phone. We dropped our hands. He looked so much the part of the keen, empathetic politician that we were momentarily at a loss for words.

"It's about Natalie. We're her best friends," we said.

"You have a wonderful friend." He smiled, revealing nice, straight teeth. "She's so driven and committed. The future of Hong Kong is bright."

"But politics is not for her. Please don't drag her into it."

"Why?" he asked, hands cupping his chin, seeming genuinely engaged in what we had to say.

We sat up, bolstered by his interest. "Because politics, and all the talk about freedom and democracy, is impractical. It won't put food on the table. It won't buy you a house. It won't give you smart, healthy kids. Does it matter who is elected and who is appointed if you can't pay your bills and mortgage? The only freedom worth talking about is financial freedom."

Our hands were trembling. Had we gone too far? But the sparkle in his eye told us we hadn't gone far enough. So we said, with an audacity surprising ourselves, "Let's be honest—you know that politics is just a show. You're here in your nice little office because you know how to entertain and capture the public interest."

He sat in silence, long enough that we began to feel afraid. Finally, he said, "And is that so bad? Capturing the public interest?" He leaned back in his chair, crossing his ankle at his knee. "I got you interested. Why else would you be in my office right now?"

"Because we want you to get Natalie to stop. You're an influential politician, right?" We leaned forward, batting our eyelash extensions like butterfly wings, hoping our eyes sparkled like Alex's. "She needs to come into her own and start living in the present instead of clinging to the past or the future or some fuzzy ideal bigger than herself. You may need the paycheck, but she doesn't. She has plenty of other opportunities."

"You think politics is impractical." He chewed over our words, his eyebrows stitching into a frown of mockery and concern. "So is there anything you find practical? Besides money?"

"Yes, of course." We disliked the perfunctory way he'd made that assumption. Had Natalie talked that way about us? "Friendship, for example. We care about Natalie. If you really cared about her, you wouldn't want her to go down this path."

"You think friendship is practical?" He laughed, and our faces warmed.

"Well, not practical, but concrete. Safe."

"Interesting," he said, folding up the sleeves of his shirt. "To me, relationships are the least concrete thing. People always change. Politics, on the other hand, involves concrete, attainable demands. It's also practical." He laughed again and cracked his knuckles. Glancing at the clock on the wall, he said, "Anyway, thank you for coming in today. I understand your concern. I think you're right, though—Natalie does need to come into her own. Let me talk to her."

He stood, but we were reluctant to get up from our seats. There was much more to say about Natalie. Were the rumors in the papers true? Were they sleeping together? How serious were they? But he was already at the door, holding it open for us like a gentleman.

We said goodbye, disappointed he hadn't asked us anything about our lives, as though we were just another constituent he had to serve. Given our relationship with Natalie, we thought he'd be more interested in getting to know us. But at least he promised to talk to her. Before he turned back into his room, we were struck by the way he rubbed his eyes with the back of his hands, the same way our babies did when they were tired or in great discomfort.

We knew we had done the right thing, and yet, as we passed the scowling secretary on our way out, we couldn't shake the lingering guilt that we'd somehow betrayed Natalie by meeting with Alex behind her back. And what bothered us most was that we didn't dislike Alex. Despite the unconventional way he made a living, he almost seemed normal, compassionate and nice-smelling, another puzzle piece we could fit into our lives: an extra place mat at dinner parties next to our husbands, a marriage for our Natalie, another chance to slip into a uniform of bridesmaid dresses, filing down the aisle in a beautiful, measured procession of order, clinging to the promise of a bright successful future, just like we used to.

SEVERAL WEEKS AFTER our visit to Alex's, we were on our way to see a movie—*Little Women*—when we got a text from Natalie's mother. The last time we'd tried to see the movie, our bus had been stalled by one of the large anti-government protests that were becoming more and more commonplace. Surrounded by an angry swarm of protesters who had spilled out onto the road, chanting for democracy, we scrolled through Facebook and watched sappy Korean dramas until our phones died. Two hours later, the same protesters, with their black outfits and pink gas masks, piled onto our bus and we were able to get going again. The cinema had been forced to shut down to accommodate the protests, but we were able to exchange our tickets.

The text asked us to come visit as soon as we could: Natalie was losing her mind. We smiled knowingly at each other, victorious. Alex had talked to her after all, and Natalie would soon be returned to us. Instead of heading to the theater, we turned around and set off for her family's apartment.

When we arrived, Natalie's mother opened the door for us. Natalie's potbellied father was sitting in a brown leather armchair in the living room, a scowl on his face, newspaper held out in front of him with the headline NEW SECURITY LAW TO STOP PROTESTS. He didn't look up. Next to him was the teddy bear cabinet we'd stood in front of and admired on our childhood visits. Yet, as we tiptoed past him, we felt for the first time the cruelty of taking what belonged in a child's arms and locking it behind a glass case. The teddy bears sat in rows, cold and aloof, in sore need of a kid's squeeze, a toy stethoscope placed on their hearts, or a teacup lifted to their lips—though, strangely, none of his creations had mouths. Natalie's mother ushered us through the living room, past a pair of Qing Dynasty vases that were taller than us, down the hallway hung with family portraits, and into Natalie's room.

Natalie was standing by the window, seemingly fixated on the adjacent block of cement apartments, which were identical to hers. Books and papers were scattered in a chaotic jumble on her desk, and clothes were piled up like ant mounds on the bed and carpet.

"Have you heard about the new national security law? It's so scary," she said, turning around as we entered.

Laws were passed all the time; how could we keep up? Besides, they were only important to those who intended to break them. "Hello to you, too."

Despite her thin limbs, her cheeks were still as chubby and cherubic as the day she'd barged in on our conversation and our lives all those years ago. She didn't seem surprised to see us.

She told us to sit and asked if we wanted anything to drink, without any real intention of moving away from the window. We flicked loose underwear out of the way so we could sit on her bed. A girl's room shouldn't be such a mess, we thought. It reflected a flawed character. We wondered if her mother had fired their housekeeper or something.

Settling into our positions on the bed, we waited for the accusations to fly. We'd decided that the best way to deal with Natalie's anger for going behind her back was to stay silent. In time, she would understand we'd only wanted the best for her.

Natalie stepped away from the window, pushed some papers out of the way, and propped herself up onto the desk, legs dangling. "I've decided to run in the upcoming elections," she said.

"What?"

"I've done enough observing from the sidelines. I want to play my part in fighting for democracy in Hong Kong. I'm going to run as a representative of the Social Democratic Party." She beamed proudly.

Dread filled our chests. It was like those university clubs all over again. "Is this because of Alex?"

"He said it's time for the next generation to take the helm and for old men like him to step aside. He's going to let me run. But I've also been thinking about this for a long time. How to contribute in a more concrete way." She picked up a piece of paper and began folding it.

Our hearts pounded. Alex had lied to us. We couldn't believe we had fallen for his charms. "Do you need a job? We can help make referrals."

Natalie laughed and shook her head. "It's definitely not about the job. I want to help and do something for our city."

We began to lose our patience. "Why do you always have to think about others, Natalie? Why can't you think about yourself for once?"

"This is the most selfish thing I've ever done in my life. It *is* for myself."

"But what about your actual life? Don't you want to find a guy, start a family of your own, settle down like us?"

"Oh, I'm way ahead of you. I have two kids already with Alex." She smirked, her hands still busy folding paper.

We couldn't decide whether she was joking or being immature. "So you're really dating him? The newspapers weren't lying? What about his wife?"

"Ex-wife. And don't change the subject. What do you think? Will you help me campaign?" She looked expectantly at us.

So it was true. "We don't like Alex. He's a hypocrite. Seriously, do you know how old he is?" We remembered the drooling girls on his desk. "You're going to take care of his babies?"

Natalie threw back her head, laughing. "His babies are teenagers. They're nice girls."

"So you're going to mother two teenage girls?" We couldn't believe our ears. How could she skip all the rites of passage to motherhood—the wedding stress and pregnancy fat and parent handbooks and hair loss and sore, cracked nipples and playgroup research—and claim it was the same thing? It just wouldn't be fair to us.

"If you help me campaign, you can get to know Alex a little bit better. He doesn't shout and throw things in real life, I promise."

That's why he's a hypocrite, we thought.

She smoothed out the edges of her paper, revealing an airplane. She grinned and launched it at us. "And so you can understand what I do, too," she added. "It would be good to stop thinking about yourselves for once."

Natalie's accusation cut deep. She wore the same patronizing smirk as Alex had. They shouted slogans, waved banners, and thought they were better than everyone with real jobs. We wanted to tell her we had met Alex and knew enough about him already. But there was no point in arguing with her. She was not well.

As we filed out through the living room, Natalie's mom jumped up expectantly. We shook our heads, and her face fell. Natalie's father, still staring at his papers, let out a small grunt. An inexplicable anger welled up in us. He was leaning into his armchair like he was king of all the teddy bears, resentful that we hadn't offered gifts at his feet. And then, like the crack of an egg, a pocket of clarity opened in us. *He* was at fault, he was to blame for all this. It was his money, his business, his practicality against which our friend was rebelling. He was her target, not us. Alex, politics, the elections—they were just the latest weapons in their battle. Because of him, we'd wasted our tickets for *Little Women*.

We were too preoccupied with our own anger to have noticed it then: how odd it was that Natalie never brought up our visit with Alex.

WHEN OUR PHONES lit up with breaking news that the pro-democrats who had run in the elections were being arrested under the new national security law for attempting to overthrow the government, we were not surprised to find in the link a recent picture of Natalie, handing out election pamphlets on the street in a white-green floral-print dress. She had a sheepish look on her face, as though embarrassed by the self-promotion. For the first time in our lives, we began following the news on Facebook: Natalie's application for bail was denied due to the high risk of her defecting. No one knew when her hearing would be. Cases of national security were tried without juries. Her sentence would likely range from three years to life imprisonment. "But she lost the election," we typed in one Facebook discussion, then deleted, in fear of it being traced back to us. We were not political.

Natalie was locked away in a prison in the New Territories, close to the border with China. We found ourselves on a two-hour journey to visit her, taking the subway, then a train, then a minivan. Slowly, the narrow one-way streets filled with pedestrians widened into busy cross-town highways before turning off onto dirt roads dotted with grazing cows.

In our tote bags were the supplies Natalie's mother had asked us to buy, following the instructions on the prison website. Body wash: *Johnson's baby bath. 750ml. Transparent blue bottle. One every two months.* Hair tie: *4 x 0.3cm. Red. No pattern. Single loop. Plastic. Six per month.* M&M's: *37g. Black or yellow packaging. Five packets per visit.* The prison must have forgotten to update the website— we looked all over town for the discontinued sanitary napkins: *Whisper. Instant Clean Slim Night Wing. 12's. 28 cm.*

Natalie had also requested some books on politics—*On Tyranny, 1984, The People's Republic of Amnesia*—six, the maximum allowed. Thirteen years at Saint Theresa's had failed to convert us, but we snuck in a couple religious books: *Doing Time with God* and *The Purpose Driven Life.* There was no limit on the number of religious books allowed.

There had been doubts about making the trip. By visiting her, would we be associating ourselves with criminals? Might we be seen as a threat to national security ourselves? Were the names of visitors being recorded and filed?

In the tote bag was also a printed email from Alex, received shortly after Natalie's bail was denied. After reading it, we knew we had to go.

Angie,

Hope this email finds you well. I got your contact from the business card you left with my secretary. This may seem sort of sudden, but I am now in London, applying for refugee status. With the situation developing in Hong Kong, it's only a matter of time before they come after me. I wanted to let you know—to let Natalie know, actually—that I don't know when I will be back. With kids and all—I'm sure you understand. A public announcement is in the works, but for now, I'm going to lie low for a little while. I know Natalie is going through a rough patch. I have no way of contacting her so please send her my regards when you visit.

It's good to know she has you girls to support her. Perhaps the friendship
you talked about might assert itself—both concrete and practical. Take
care of her for me.

    Hope all is well in HK,
    Alex

AT THE PRISON entrance, the Chinese and Hong Kong flags
flapped violently side by side in the wind. We looked up at them for
a moment and felt immediately calmer. It was just like going back
to school. We stored our Chanel bags in the free lockers, passed
through metal detectors, and showed identification. We were led
through a long white hallway lined with switched-off fans and
heavily padlocked doors, constantly buzzing and shutting behind
us. We reached another checkpoint for submitting the supplies we
brought for Natalie and were asked yet again for identification. The
irritation must have aired on our faces, because the security guard,
taking our IDs with long, sooty fingers, whispered with a smirk,
"You want your pussy searched like the prisoners?" Instinctively,
we looked behind our shoulders, but there was no one there. He let
us through the checkpoint, but his sneer, the most alive thing we'd
seen all day, was seared into our memories. We thought of him
often, his dirty fingers prying us open, worming their way into us,
searching for what we didn't know was missing, the ingredient that
made all the difference between us and Natalie.

    In the visiting room, we sat on round metal stools in front of the
double-glazed glass. Beads of sweat trickled down our chests as we
waited for Natalie to arrive. We took out the email we'd printed,
passed it around yet again. When we went to see Alex that day in

his office, had he been planning his escape already? Was this why he asked Natalie to run in the elections in his place and why he never told her of our visit? Or was he simply trying to save our friendship? Sure, his behavior was wild and uncivilized, his job unorthodox, but did that qualify him for refugee status? We reread his sentence over and over again: *With kids and all—I'm sure you understand.* The thing was, we did. Completely. More so than Natalie ever would. He was just looking out for his daughters, the same way we would. Natalie was the collateral damage, the sacrificial lamb.

There were more things we wanted to update Natalie on: Angie's second pregnancy, Bernadette's miscarriage, Clara's cancer scare, and the birthday party we just threw for Denise's baby boy. A new molecular-fusion restaurant had just opened in Soho, one of the best meals we'd ever had. We wanted to bring Natalie there. We knew she would hate it, questioning why we would waste so much money, money she'd never have, for foie gras to taste like durian ice cream, or for enormous plates to hold a spoonful of caviar that looked like frog spawn, adorned with white foam resembling an old man's spittle. We just wanted to see her face when she said it, all scrunched up with self-righteousness, to remind us of the girl we once knew.

When the buzzing doors opened and Natalie walked over to our booth on the other side of the glass, we tried not to stare.

Her bare face. Her low ponytail tied up with a red plastic band. Her slender frame, even skinnier in the oversize brown plaited uniform. Her thin wrists, too small for the large metal cuffs, which the security guard unlocked when she sat down. "Phone!" she mouthed and pointed through the glass, so we picked up the white receiver on the counter in front of us.

We straightened out the email in our hands, but Natalie began gushing about prison life like an overexcited child.

"Did you know that we wake at six thirty, exercise at seven, shower at six, eat at seven, and sleep at ten? I've been doing so much exercise and lost weight. Did you know the best food in prison is the oranges? The scrambled eggs are pretty decent, too. I'm taking cooking lessons. We made a chocolate cake yesterday. Sewing too. I sewed a teddy bear—last week, I think. I'm becoming my father." She laughed and we shifted uncomfortably in our seats. "One day just merges into the next. There's no concept of hours or days. It's pretty weird."

We thought about our beautiful homes, our generally wonderful husbands, and the lives growing inside and outside us. We thought about the hard work and discipline we'd had to put in, the parts of ourselves we'd had to give up, to create all this beauty. So the irony was not lost on us that it was Natalie, with her grand impractical pursuits, who ended up having the most stable and orderly life. A life that automatically put meals on the table, M&M's by her bedside, visitors at her doorstep. A life that set aside time for exercise, cooking, and sewing. A life in which she didn't even have to worry about buying her own clothes and hair ties.

The more she raved about prison, though, the more we suspected that she was preempting us. Painting a rosy picture to thwart our criticisms; taking away our time to talk so she wouldn't have to hear about our lives; proving that she was still somehow on higher ground. Regardless, we hoped this discipline would fix Natalie, right whatever was wrong with her, so she could come back out soon and be one of us again.

"Oh, you'll be interested in this," she said, eyes twinkling with mischief. "A cellmate of mine just got married in prison. Did you know you could do that? The groom and their families were waiting in a room, and she was walked in and given away by the guard. She was allowed to wear a wedding dress and exchange rings. But afterwards, they took her ring away and brought her back for dinner in prison uniform, just in time to eat scrambled eggs with us." She laughed. "I should let Alex know."

We tightened up. "About Alex—"

"I know, I know you don't like him. Let's not waste time talking about him today. I know he needs to lie low with all the fear and arrests going on. I saw from the news that everything's dissolving, even the university's students' union. I wonder what he'll do with the party, it must be such a difficult decision to make. I really don't envy him. Anyway, I know he'll come visit when he's ready." She spoke faster and faster, barely pausing between thoughts. She must have harbored her own theories as to why Alex hadn't come to see her.

Our hearts sank. We fumbled with the email below the countertop. Alex had asked us to deliver the message; we had a responsibility to him. More importantly, here was the opportunity we'd waited for all these years—to say *We told you so*, with hard evidence in our hands, as concrete as it could be. Higher causes were nice to have, but at the end of the day, everyone looked out for themselves. We imagined the smugness unraveling on her face as we wallowed in triumph, vindicated. We would see how much she still enjoyed her cooking class then.

Instead, we blurted out the most impractical question we'd ever asked: "Are you happy here?"

She looked at us, eyes widening with surprise, and for the first time, she seemed to struggle to answer her own grand philosophical questions. "You know, in a way it's easier being in here, knowing you tried. It's almost like a recognition that they see you as a threat, meaning you had the ability to change things. So, in a strange way, I am."

We couldn't tell whether she was trying to convince herself or if she sincerely believed in what she was saying. She was free from Alex, free from her father, free from anyone else's influence. Our instinct was to clap back at her naivete, at how her lofty, impractical beliefs had landed her in trouble, but we hesitated. Some of us began to wonder if she was right: she was locked away from the world because she had the ability to change things, and it was *our* refusal to change the way we viewed her, as a child who needed to be disciplined and shaped in our likeness, that had made her threatening—until it was just simpler to have her put away so we wouldn't have to acknowledge that what she was threatening was our success.

The guard behind her signaled that our time was up. Natalie said, "Write to me. Don't mention the dreams you've had or how to escape prison, otherwise they'll confiscate the letter. And don't put anything you don't want them to know about you." The phone clicked dead.

Handcuffed again by the guard, Natalie was escorted away, smiling wryly, as though it amused her to imagine that we might have anything to hide. We folded away the email and put it back in our pockets. Perhaps next time.

We stepped out of prison into the blinding brightness, the buzz and the click of the last door behind us. We were greeted by the familiar smells of wild grass and cow manure and dry dirt kicked up by the cars driving by. We inhaled deeply.

The four of us stood in silence, watching as the red sun bled, trying to remember when we'd last looked up at the sky. Before long, it had sunk into the spikes of the prison's barbed-wire fence, beyond our sight. We wished we could go back in time, to stand once more upon the precipice of change, when everything new was a wonder and all that was required of us was that we stand in line, hoist a flag, and practice calligraphy. To a time when Natalie might still be tamed and taught to follow rules, before she had evolved into a deviant that needed to be regulated and corrected. We wondered how it was that Natalie was the one in prison, while we had somehow ended up bearing the weight of her guilt.

Leanne Ma received an MFA in fiction from UMass Boston, where she was also a teaching fellow. Her work has been published in *Salamander* and *Gulf Coast* and nominated for the Pushcart Prize. Originally from Hong Kong, she now lives in Brooklyn, New York.

Editor's Note

A salt-stained military uniform, a morose tropical island, an aged and proud political prisoner. In "Patience," by Benjamin Van Voorhis, we don't get many details, but we are awash in its distinct, singular vibe. Van Voorhis transports us to this unnamed military prison, where the leader of a failed coup is being held and left, simply, to wait. With power and glory firmly in his past, he takes long walks, plays cards, and, one day, has a conversation with one of his attendants that irrevocably alters his reality. The language and tone have the same slow, suspenseful dawning on the reader that the aftermath of this conversation has on the General. It's writing that draws you in, that asks you to linger—to reread a sentence or passage to make sure you fully appreciate what's being said, that you haven't missed any clues. The kind of writing that requires a bit of, yes, patience, from the reader—but is all the more rewarding for it. Mysterious, canny, and poignant, "Patience" will leave you feeling like you've just woken from a dream, one that you can't help but close your eyes and try to return to.

Katie Sticca, Managing Editor

Salamander

Patience

Benjamin Van Voorhis

AT HIGH TIDE THE WATER SPEWED AGAINST THE toothy outcrops and matted scrubs of the low cliff around the inlet, and not for the first time the General was reminded of a huge serrated blade, the kind you'd use to cut bread. He'd taken to walking the shore in full regalia, now defunct, all epaulets and medals and little brass clasps embossed with some Latin phrase or another. He couldn't keep them all straight anymore. The men in the garrison looked at him with the kind of pity you'd reserve for the ancient and the insane, but he wore it anyway, the regalia, sometimes baking under the woolen weight of his uniform, sodden with ocean spray that salted the patchy beard he'd let root on his cheeks these last years.

In the first days of exile, he'd worn his regalia because he wanted to be ready. If his supporters came for him or he found a way of escape, well, you wanted a full-splendor thing going on, a sense that you hadn't diminished, that you could still fit, so to speak, into your boots. But no one had come, and the years had gone by, and in fact he had diminished. Meaning that incident a year ago or more with the collapsed vertebrae, when they'd got some renowned Welsh surgeon to come out and inflate a balloon in his spine, or so he understood. Though the procedure alleviated his crushing pain and enabled him to walk, he came out of it two full humiliating inches down. So he supposed the question of the regalia was now one of habit, of long-ingrained decorum. All that was left was schedule and routine and ceremony.

The rocks bit his booted feet, and he steadied himself against the hickory cane. It was unusually nippy, but he was sweating anyway, and his left heel felt like it had grown an extra tarsal. His insignias jangled as he went. Waves crashed the time. Clouds scudded sunward. He'd been in the habit of trying to raise his head when he walked, but it was so difficult on uneven ground that he'd learned to bow, eyes always on the shoes. Even so, they were almost crinkled shut from the force of the wind, which of course never stopped blowing. The kind of wind that leaves your eyeballs dune-dry.

The trail on the scarp looped a little over four miles along the shoreline and back into the forest with its tangled growth and wide-fronded trees before cutting up a steep slope to Breton House, all pressed between ocean and the long-dormant volcano in the middle of the island. Coming back around the loop to approach the house, he always felt some mixture of bitterness and relief. Can a home really be home if you don't choose it? But of course it can; children don't choose their homes. Maybe it was that you had to resent being treated like a child—despite the renowned intellect and power he wasn't sure he possessed anymore, or ever did.

Breton House was less a house than a mansion, all wide entryway with its huge green latticework and whitewashed double doors. A low stone wall crept around the grounds, and the path was lined by agapanthus. One of his attendants did most of the garden-tending, although the General had more than once come out to prune some of the bushes around the sides of the house or pick mangoes from the rear orchard, and had always thought of it as a decent way to pass the time, which of course was what mattered.

The flag of his country was raised on the grounds beside the flag of the country that had taken him captive. Flailing in the wind, they looked like the same flag, only with the colors all jumbled up.

Sergeant Hullum was at attention by the door when the General shuffled up the rough dirt path and across the grass, and fingered his temple by way of salute. The General shook his head, admonishing; Hullum's pleasant expression wavered.

As the General pulled himself up the stone veranda steps, Hullum said, "Lieutenant Deluca was looking for you, sir—I mean—well, he was looking for you, that's all."

"Looking?" said the General. A light fog was starting to drape in over the shoulder of the ridge and would probably be gone in an hour or so.

Deluca wanted to relate something to the General, Hullum explained, then asked whether the General would receive him in the study, as he often did. The General nodded stiffly, then slipped inside the creaking doors without reply.

OF ALL THE things you could do to pass the time, the best was cards. Prior to his exile, the General hadn't been so fond of card games, but solitude will turn your likes and dislikes on their heads. You think of time as really meaning something until it's all you have. There's a difference, after all, between passing time and time passing you. He thought, for instance, of all those war councils and diplomatic liaisons in the Mason Room at the Presidential Palace, so named because there had once been a president in that country before the General ousted him. He'd kept every appointment he ever made, to the best of his recollection, because he'd always understood that time only means anything when you impose a structure on it—in other words, when it's made up of appointments. Each inter-appointment period spent waiting for the next one. Now there were no appointments, now he spent every moment in a state of waiting. The only appointment he was waiting for was the last one, the one you didn't come back from.

All this being why he passed so much time these days playing cards, both with the men in the garrison and by himself, dredging up the patience games his brother used to play when he contracted tuberculosis as a child. The men had brought over a thick, scratched-up mahogany table that now leaned slightly in the middle of the study on which he'd taught his gaolers quadrille with a deck of tattered, salt-coarse, comically small playing cards. The thing about the men was they bored easily. The General, however, was the type who could focus on any one thing for as long as necessary. In his own estimation, it was what made him an effective commander and governor.

Though the table had always leaned, now it was really wobbly. The General kept sticking thin volumes under one of the legs only to have need of them later and be left with a tilting table once again. At those times, he imagined it was the room that was tilted rather than the table itself. He'd taken off his jacket and hat and polished leather belt, now only in his shirtsleeves and trousers undone to give his gut some breathing room. The study smelled sort of musty these days, even when he kept the door open, and the windows rattled with the constant gust, and the floors were always slightly damp. He groaned into the secondhand chair at the card table and shuffled, mulling over the Deluca thing. Of the men, it was Lieutenant Deluca he was friendliest with. They'd struck up a rapport during the course of an almost accidental series of English lessons, which was doubly odd since Deluca was Italian by birth. But no gaoler nor any of his attendants had ever left a message that he was looked-for, and it bothered him.

The cards had been thumbed so thoroughly that many had lost corners and their edges were faded and watery, but he liked the feel of them in his hands, matte and pliable. He dealt. The thing about this particular variation of patience was that it forced you to think. Sometimes he might stare at a configuration for some minutes before finding a pattern, or drawing from the stock, and often there was no way out. As a boy this had frustrated him, and even more recently, at the start of his exile, it was tough to muster the will to let the solution come to him, or to realize there was no solution at all, that he'd dealt a bad game. Meaning, of course, a static one, on which you couldn't impose any sense of order. This was a conclusion he'd come to lately, that there really wasn't such a thing as a bad game, because the process of play was what mattered, and whether you won or not was only a question of variability. If there was such a thing as a bad game, though, that was what he'd dealt. He was maybe a quarter through the stock already and had only uncovered a couple of aces by the time someone knocked on the door and the General said to come in.

Entering, Deluca was all matted black curls and long face, glass eye squeaking disconcertingly in its socket, unable to quite keep up with the movement of its owner's head. He carried a small paper-and-twine-wrapped package under his arm. As always, his uniform was somewhat disheveled, as in trousers untucked from boots, as in mismatched buttonry. But the General wouldn't scold another man's solider for his dress, as much as he'd like to. Deluca had the habit of grinning with every muscle in his cheeks, like he was constipated or something, and he did this now seeing the General hunched over his game of patience. "This again?" His voice was all skin and bones, a breathy whistle.

The General nearly smiled but didn't. "Hullum told that you had a message."

"Said," corrected Deluca.

"Yes, he said so."

"It's more of a gift, really," said Deluca, foisting the package with what seemed to the General an unnecessary flourish. "Voilà, mon commandant!" He set it on the table where the vacant foundations had yet to be placed and leaned back with a beam. The General didn't admonish him for addressing him wrongly; already his tacit chastisement of the sergeant that morning seemed foolish and out of order.

"What is it?" he asked. The monthly shipment must have come in from San Lucia, maybe yesterday, maybe this morning. It unnerved him that he'd lost track of the days like that.

With a touch of good-natured impatience, Deluca said, "Well, open it!"

The General gingered his fingers underneath the twine and pulled. The wrapping was stiff enough with wax and salt that the whole thing just about sprang open to reveal a wooden box that professed in ornate stamped lettering to contain ten packs of handmade Ptolemy playing cards. God knew how much someone had paid for these. The box itself was ornately crafted as well, jointed immaculately at the corners and painted with little abstract, angular designs. Even the brass latch was fashioned into the shape of a shell, its texture undulous to the touch. For some reason, this brought to mind the palaces and mansions he'd lived in even as a boy, since his parents, too, were members of the court. Every silk sheet and high-collared shirt and handmade toy soldier he'd ever owned, every imported cigar or pen or piece of china, every commissioned portrait, every unearned badge and title. He wanted to be grateful—elated, even—at the sight of the box, he wanted to envision the crisp cards inside, but all he felt was a sort of vague disgust. It must've come across on his face, because Deluca faltered somewhat, lips twitching. "Don't you like it?"

Quickly the General put on a tired smile. "Yes, in fact," he said, unclasping the box, examining the rows of brightly painted packages. "It is an admirable thing."

If he expected Deluca to react favorably, he was disappointed. The lieutenant's face fell even more, one eye flicking away while the other remained focused on the General, who kept up a neutral expression despite his unease.

Deluca finally spoke. "Even in my country you have your supporters, you know. People who thought you had the right idea. We're all lagging behind, and you . . . The future doesn't wait, one could say. He was a brute, the president of your country. Before his head . . . well . . ." He briefly raspberried, which seemed both inappropriate and inaccurate.

The General's stomach rose and fell at the same time, a weird combination of excitement and dread. "That's dangerous talk."

Deluca twisted one of his rings like he was trying to start a fire. "It's important to do what's good, isn't it?"

"I don't know a person who would disagree."

This time Deluca waited so long to speak the General thought he might have fallen asleep. Eyes shut and everything, breathing even as a metronome. The sound of it somewhat unsettling.

"They cut me, you know. When I was a boy." Deluca opened his eyes slowly. He extracted a pack of the crisp, new playing cards and spun it in his fingers as he spoke. "I had a nice voice." He nearly whispered this last thing.

The General didn't know what to make of that. "Your parents, or . . . ?"

"I had an effusive, rich music teacher. He offered to buy me, in effect."

"How many years did you have?"

Deluca thought for a second. "Nine, I think. Or ten."

"And you were good?"

"I was very good."

Deluca wasn't looking at him anymore with either eye. Something strained between them, maybe something unsaid that needed to be said or something that shouldn't be said at all. The General imagined this soldier as a boy, hair wigged and powdered, resplendent in something stuffy and high-collared and pearl-blue, looking like a doll stuffed into adult-human clothing, mouth agape, teeth straight, belting some aria written for a castrato, maybe specifically for him, to take advantage of his talents. Stunted, wounded. And of course, still with the glass eye, which the General had never asked him about. There was something in the way he'd said it, the thing about being very good, that made the General feel as though quality wasn't what mattered at all, that Deluca as a boy had never thought of quality, not when everyone else was doing the thinking for him, his parents, his teacher. He'd been helpless in that life, and then he was a soldier, a cast-aside one, gaoler of an old man in this moldy house in the middle of the sea.

Deluca reached down to draw a card from one of the General's foundations, the two of clubs, and looked at it like it was something precious with its ragged corners. He seemed to be making a huge and consequential decision. You could tell, often, about decisions like that. The General had seen enough men make huge and consequential decisions in his career—whether to bombard this fortification or that one, to kill by guillotine or firing squad or some other monstrous method. Wasn't every method monstrous when it came to death? But the decision was still a huge and consequential one, and you could tell by the way the jaw locked into place, the quick intake of breath, the clenching and unclenching of the fleshy knuckles. In the quiet you could hear men raucousing from the barracks on the other side of the grounds, gulls shrieking overhead, maybe if you strained even the whipping of flags in the wind. For a split second, Deluca's eyes seemed to bulge in their sockets, so quick the General wasn't sure he'd seen it at all. Then his face settled into an easy smile, and the card went back on the foundation.

"Forgive the intrusion," Deluca said finally. There was something off about him now, shale-faced. "I hope you enjoy the gift. I hope you think of it as a good one."

And before the General could reassure him, tell him it was a good gift, or reflect on his impulse to reassure a foreign soldier, an enemy of the state and his own gaoler, to think first of his dignity and composure, Deluca had basically fled the room. The General watched the open doorway for a minute, listening to Deluca's footfalls rebound down the creaky hallway. Then he placed the new pack of Ptolemy playing cards back in its exquisite box, clasped it shut, and gently carried the box to the writing desk in the corner of the room. He sat back down at the mahogany table and resumed his game.

THE GENERAL HAD plenty of opportunity that afternoon to reflect on the conversation, which was so odd as to be practically alarming, and it alarmed him right up until he limped to his bedroom on the second floor to retrieve his reading glasses and found a neatly folded piece of paper tucked beneath his pillowcase which read only *Second kitchen door, one o'clock, morning*. Of course the General understood then, how could he not have seen it before, that Deluca not only saw eye to eye with his politics but wanted to act on it, to get him off this rock. Here was proof that the world hadn't forgotten him. He expected again to feel that sense of elation he'd felt when he sat on the throne of his country the first time, not as its inheritor or elect, but as its conqueror, a bloodless coup until he bloodied it, and kept bloodying. The bellyache of pride he felt when the president's noggin sheared off the other side of the bascule and came to rest open-eyed. Only he couldn't conjure that pride now, not even something as strong as regret. He was just thin, hollowed out. What he did feel was a swelling tenderness for Deluca, who, after all, was risking not only his position but his life for the General. It was hard to fathom, that someone could do so much for a person to whom they owed so little.

The General sat down on his slab of a mattress, whose sheets were crumpled and coarse and made him sweat no matter how cold it was at night. He tried to recall if he'd met any castrati in his own country or if he'd ever implicitly condoned such a process or a process like it. It was hard for him to imagine, not only the physical pain of it, but the lingering of it, the gnawing absence of what made you a man, made you into something you weren't and could never be. At first he thought it was a little like his current scenario, having constructed himself and his career in a particular way only to be stripped of it, of every office and lick of goodwill—but it wasn't like that at all, not even a little. The body was precious, and to treat it with such frivolous cruelty . . . ? Deluca was good, he'd said, very good. No, it wasn't the same thing at all.

One time, the General had held a conversation with a traitor to his country. The man was shackled to a cell wall pockmarked with traces of bloodied fingernails and holes through which rats wriggled. There was a small wooden bench, but the shackles were so high up he couldn't sit. He'd pissed himself more than once, and the wall behind him was stained with shit. His clothes were ragged and colorless, beard the texture of goat's hair and studded with sores. The smell was so unbearable it made you choke. The General showed up right on time for the appointment but couldn't remember what the man had done to end up in hell except that he was a traitor, that he'd aided and abetted some foreign enemy, that he wanted to undermine the General, and the General had come because the traitor's last request was to speak with him, and though his advisers thought it was a stupid idea, he'd been curious and acquiesced.

The traitor laughed when he saw the General. He was surprised that the General had deigned to give him an audience. Those were his exact words, "deigned" and "audience," and he of course said them bitingly. His accent was aristocratic. You'd think he just had a bad cold, the way his throat rasped when he spoke. The General asked him what he wanted as part of his last request, whether to beg for his life or to ask some favor for his family. The traitor shook his head. "I just thought you should see," he said. "I wanted you to look." Then he started to laugh, like the thing he'd said was so hilarious you wouldn't believe, but he was also crying, in fact he was sobbing, these chest-heaving sobs that shook his gutted ribs like a piston, and in between sobs he was saying, "I'm here," and "Here I am," and the General couldn't look away, not until his armed escort pulled him by the bicep out of the vulgar-smelling chamber and down the maze of the prison halls until he could taste sunlight again.

The traitor was executed by firing squad the following week, and for a long time after, the General dreamed about him. In his dreams, the traitor was suspended in the air above a field of wildflowers rippling in wind, arms outstretched and head tilted and thorn-crowned like Jesus on the cross, and he wept silently. The tears tracked down his cheeks. He was trying to say something, but the General was too far away to hear, and it hurt so much to walk he could never quite make it in time. The traitor was gone by the time the General approached him, as if he'd never been there in the first place.

A LITTLE AFTER midnight, the General packed what little he thought he couldn't live without into a mottled knapsack: the insignia-emblazoned knife he'd always carried as a commander on the field, a few books of physics and philosophy and an English newspaper dated the previous month, a pocket-watch, a set of reliable pens and a water-scarred notebook, some letters, a small retractable brass telescope, and of course the box of Ptolemy playing cards from the study, although to be honest, he couldn't imagine playing patience aboard a ship, the slick cards shifting around with the motion of the waves. Just to be sure, he packed the old, tattered deck as well. He thought a long time about whether to wear his regalia. It's hard to break a habit, after all, and how would the people receive him without it?

Throughout the evening, the General had tried unsuccessfully to recall a sense of excitement or relief, and at first he thought it was the nerves getting to him, that he was just so anxious about the process of escape that he had no room for the prospect itself to sink in, that once he was through the second kitchen door, it would be smooth sailing. But something was off-center in him. He was thinking more and more about Deluca having been cut as a child, and the traitor's body hanging in the wind, and what was forming instead of excitement was a vast pit. It was his tenderness for Deluca, however, the gesture with the Ptolemy playing cards, that made the General keep to the instructions laid out by the note, to don his regalia and make his way quietly out of the study and down the hall.

The kitchen had three doors—one at the terminus of the hall adjacent to the foyer, one around the side, just down the stairs from the study, and one around the back, which his attendants primarily used. Even at this hour there were guards, though he and they had been on the island so long without incident that complacency was the general rule, meaning there might be a couple, at most, posted in the foyer. Even so, he made sure to step light, and carried the hickory cane at his side instead of supporting himself with it. As a consequence, he limped down the hall from the study, then down the side-stairs leading to the kitchen door. He took small steps and shuffled with his bad foot to avoid setting off the floorboards and to prevent his regalia from making noise. Now he regretted having worn it. He felt silly and self-important and small.

Partway down the stairs he stopped, letting his eyes adjust to the moonbeams bathing the hall below. You could just see the kitchen door from this angle. No one was there. He checked his pocket-watch, having to tilt it downward to catch the light through the windows, and saw he was right on time. Of course, the note hadn't specified which side of the door he needed to be on, and he suspected they'd leave from the kitchen anyway. There was an entrance to the storm cellar there, and tunnels you might take to retrieve grain or travel surreptitiously to different parts of the grounds. He went on, forgetting to skip the fifth step up.

The moment his weight came down, the wood caterwauled like an infant, shrieking each way down the hall; it was a miracle the whole of Breton House didn't come alive then, soldiers descending on him like he was carrion. Heart thrashing, the General flicked through every possibility—that Deluca would burst through the kitchen door and pull him dramatically to safety, that one of his attendants would come out to see what all the noise was about, that a pair of gaolers would rush around the corner behind the stairs and spot him trying to make a break for it, in which case he'd have to come up with a story—sleepwalking, the early onset of senility, something like that. But nobody came, and his heartbeat evened, and then it was so quiet you could hear his pocket-watch ticking away. The next step didn't creak, nor did the last few.

At the kitchen door, the General paused. It was the wrong shape.

He wouldn't have been able to explain why this thought occurred to him; it was the same door it had always been, deep brown and rectangular and embossed with four smaller rectangles, themselves embossed with twisting floral patterns, and sporting a heavy brass knob that was dented on the left side and shone with dull moonlight. All the same, it was wrong. He wouldn't be able to fit through. Yes, but not because the door was the wrong shape. It was only him, tilted and out of proportion. Maybe a year ago he might have been able to go through, maybe two years. It was hard to say when the change had occurred, or when he'd become aware of it. Maybe it wasn't a singular change, but the culmination of ten thousand different changes all stacked on top of one another, and maybe his noticing had been just as gradual, the disease of the shape which wouldn't allow him through the door. It would be so easy, wouldn't it, just to grasp the knob, to turn and push and vanish. But then what? Would the people welcome him cheering, arms wide? Or like an old lover, having moved on without him? The world hadn't stopped turning in his exile and neither had he. Maybe it didn't matter whether the door was the wrong shape or he was. Deluca was waiting on the other side of it, somewhere, and everyone who loved him and owed him nothing, and who loathed him with good reason, and every indifferent eye, and the vast ocean.

He turned away from the door and went a little way down the hall, where there was another door. In every respect it was identical to the second kitchen door. The crucial difference being that it was the right shape for his body. He went out of the house and into the dark. At night the trail on the scarp seemed shorter. He took a narrower path down the hill and out toward the ocean to avoid any sharp-eyed gaolers, but the going felt easier, so much so that he didn't have to use his cane for maybe a half mile, and even then its heft supported him in a way he couldn't remember it having done before. It was cold, but the weight of his regalia kept his temperature up, and his joints didn't ache much, maybe just a shallow twinge of the spine. It was a full moon, so bright he could see every rock beneath his boots. He was probably a mile out then, almost to the bread-knife inlet, when he noticed he was no longer wearing the knapsack. Maybe he'd dropped it along the trail without noticing and it was lying somewhere half-covered in dust and ants big as sugar cubes. Or maybe he'd left it just outside the second kitchen door that fit him wrong, or at the top of the stairs, or maybe it had never gone out of the study, because he knew, even then, that he couldn't bring himself to leave. Which possibly had something to do with the feel of the tilted mahogany table under his weathered hands, the smell of sea-stripped playing cards. It wasn't out of love or fear. It wasn't a bad game he'd been dealt, only a static one. He couldn't judge whether he should die or not, guillotined or executed by firing squad, or live out the rest of his lonely days here, or be castrated. How could you say what you deserved, how could anyone?

He came to the inlet now, and the tide was out. There was a gentle slope down the cliff. He stopped to take off his boots and socks before descending so he could feel the fine sand between his toes. You could hear the sound of waves like a clock. He slid onto the beach and his cane sank into the ground unsteadily so he ditched it. From near the low cliff, the flat seemed like it stretched out forever before hitting the water's edge, but he walked forward anyway, picturing the sand sprouting wildflowers, everywhere laced with them. His limp now pronounced. His feet hurt, and his back. They would never stop hurting, probably. As he went he stripped, first the jacket with its epaulets and clasps, then the iron-pressed trousers, his shirtsleeves and underthings. The air struck right through him and goose pimples broke out all along his arms and the back of his neck. His hands shook and twitched. Sand dampened underfoot. Now his feet were coated with it, and the waves were close enough for him to make out the silver froth clearly with the moon shining like that. And finally the water came up over his toes with a shock of cold. He stopped, catching his breath, naked in the shallows, imagining the schooner that was supposed to take him away, to his old life or a new one, maybe sailing empty, northward, with a skeleton crew or no crew at all, a ghost ship creaking in the waves. He stood there without knowing what he was waiting for. Maybe nothing. Only that the sea broke around his ankles, that the wind was blowing, and the tide was starting to come back in.

Benjamin Van Voorhis is a writer and musician from Santa Clarita, California. He holds an MFA in fiction from Eastern Washington University and is the former managing editor of *Willow Springs* magazine. He currently lives in Spokane, Washington.

About the Judges

SINDYA BHANOO is the author of the story collection *Seeking Fortune Elsewhere*, which won the Oregon Book Award, the New American Voices Award, and the Writers' League of Texas Book Award. Her fiction has appeared in *Granta*, *New England Review*, *Glimmer Train*, and elsewhere.

SIDIK FOFANA is the author of the story collection *Stories from the Tenants Downstairs*. His work has appeared in *The Sewanee Review* and *Granta*. He was named a fellow at the Center for Fiction in 2018.

AYŞEGÜL SAVAŞ is the author of the acclaimed novels *Walking on the Ceiling* and *White on White*. Her work has been translated into seven languages and has appeared in *The New Yorker*, *The Paris Review*, and *Granta*.

About the PEN/Robert J. Dau Short Story Prize for Emerging Writers

The PEN/Robert J. Dau Short Story Prize for Emerging Writers recognizes fiction writers for a debut short story published in a print or online literary magazine. The annual award was offered for the first time during PEN America's 2017 literary awards cycle. The winning stories are selected by a committee of three judges. The writers of the stories each receive a $2,000 cash prize and are honored at the annual PEN America Literary Awards Ceremony in New York City. Every year, Catapult publishes the winning stories in *Best Debut Short Stories: The PEN America Dau Prize*. This award is generously supported by the family of the late Robert J. Dau, whose commitment to the literary arts has made him a fitting namesake for this career-launching prize. Mr. Dau was born and raised in Petoskey, a city in Northern Michigan in close proximity to Walloon Lake, where Ernest Hemingway spent his summers as a young boy and which serves as the backdrop for his novella *The Torrents of Spring*. Petoskey is also known for being where Hemingway determined he would commit to becoming a writer. This proximity to literary history ignited the Dau family's interest in promoting emerging voices in fiction and spotlighting the next great fiction writers.

List of Participating Publications

Able Muse

AGNI

ALOCASIA

ANMLY

Apricity Magazine

Avant-Pop

beestung

Bellevue Literary Review

Bellingham Review

Black Warrior Review

Boston Review

Breakwater Review

Byline

CALYX Journal

Catamaran Literary Review

Chicago Quarterly Review

Cleaver Magazine

Cottonwood

Cream City Review

Decolonial Passage

Diary of My Leg Hair

Driftwood Press Anthology

Electric Literature's The Commuter

Exposition Review

Fairy Tale Review

FICTION

Flash Fiction Online

Foglifter Journal

Green Eggs and Hamlet

Griffith Review

Hawaiʻi Pacific Review

HEAT

Kalahari Review

Kestrel: A Journal of Literature and Art

Lady Churchill's Rosebud Wristlet

Loose Leaves (Sunflower Station Press)

McSweeney's Quarterly Concern

Michigan Quarterly Review

Mississippi Review

Mujercitos

New England Review

Nimrod International Journal

Northwest Review

Obsidian: Literature & Arts in the African Diaspora

One Story

Panorama: The Journal of Travel, Place, and Nature

Peatsmoke Journal

Ploughshares

Porter House Review

Potomac Review

PREE

Salamander

Slippery Elm

Somnium Times

Southern Humanities Review

Southwest Review

Spire Light

Split Lip Magazine

Superstition Review

swamp pink

The Baffler

The Bitchin' Kitsch (The B'K)

The Cincinnati Review

The Drift

The Fiddlehead

The Georgia Review

The Greylock Glass

The Iowa Review

The Kenyon Review

The Madison Review

The Maine Review

The Malahat Review

The Massachusetts Review

The Offing

The Rumpus

The Sewanee Review

The Southern Review

The Stinging Fly

The Summerset Review

The Yale Review

This Is Not America (or . . . is it?)

TOWER

Transition

Triangle House Review

Unpsychology Magazine
Virginia Quarterly Review
Witness Magazine
ZYZZYVA

Permissions

PEN America stands at the intersection of literature and human rights to protect open expression in the United States and worldwide. The organization champions the freedom to write, recognizing the power of the word to transform the world. Its mission is to unite writers and their allies to celebrate creative expression and defend the liberties that make it possible. Learn more at pen.org.